MY ROTTEN LOVE LIFE

LYRA WINTERS

My Rotten Love Life © 2023 by Lyra Winters. All Rights Reserved.

All rights reserved. No part of this book may be reproduced in any form or by any electronic or mechanical means, including information storage and retrieval systems, without permission in writing from the author. The only exception is by a reviewer, who may quote short excerpts in a review.

This book is a work of fiction. Names, characters, places, and incidents either are the products of the author's imagination or are used fictitiously. Any resemblance to actual persons, living or dead, events, or locales is entirely coincidental.

Editor: Jenni Gauntt

Proofreader: Bearly Vanilla Proofreading

Alpha Readers: Kelly, Sam, Jennifer, Rachel, Renee, Lorna

Beta Readers: Pat, Amy, Teeana, Shawna, Arianna, Felicia

Visit my website at lyrawinters.com

Printed in the United States of America

First Printing: February 2023

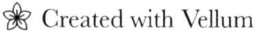

❁ Created with Vellum

AUTHOR'S NOTE

My Rotten Love Life is a whychoose romance based in the zombie apocalypse. This story *is* a whychoose romance, which means the main character will not choose between her love interests. There is no MM in this book. The romance focuses solely on the heroine of the story.

Be aware of your triggers, lovely readers. This standalone contains strong language, violence, past cheating of her ex-boyfriend and ex-best-friend, post-apocalyptic themes, amputation, infertility, endometriosis, anxiety, OCD, PTSD, euthanasia of a horse due to zombie virus, grief and loss, drama (outside of the new relationships), and explicit sexual content.

Reader's discretion is advised.

DEDICATION

Dedicated to those who like the idea of finding love in a completely devastated world.

1

TORI

It was the end of the world when I caught my best friend having sex with my boyfriend.

No, *really*.

The anguish that filled my heart as hot tears blurred my vision of them together in *our* bed was only a dull ache compared to what happened after.

I had rushed outside of our home, ignoring their attempts at explaining themselves to find the world as I knew it had ended.

A horde of zombies roamed the streets—all people I had recognized around the subdivision, very clearly dead on their feet—sinking their teeth into everyone and everything that moved.

That was three years ago.

Now, a bitter feeling swelled inside of me as I watched Jay twirl Daisy in the kitchen of my parents' cozy farmhouse, sickeningly in love. Her bare feet slapped against the white tile as she giggled, and he smiled widely at her as he brought her into his arms and hummed some old pop song.

If I was an outsider, I would've never guessed he had been my boyfriend for two years and her my best friend for fifteen years before that.

I should've taken my chances with the zombies.

Pressing my palms against the old wooden table, I moved out of my chair and slipped past them, biting my tongue as I pushed open the creaky screen door and stepped onto the patio that overlooked the ranch.

The chilly morning breeze skimmed over me, tossing my chestnut brown hair around. I shivered as I tugged the beige cardigan tighter around my body.

Summer was coming to a close, and I thought it was the end of September—not that I actually remembered. My family and I had tried to keep up with the dates, but after the second year, it all blurred together.

Days, weeks, and months were lost, and the only thing I knew for sure was that this was the third year of living at the ranch with no outside human contact.

The house was a four bedroom, two bath, and it had everything we needed and more. My parents had been living off-grid in their home long before the apocalypse. We were completely self-sustaining, and while it was annoying growing up, I was so grateful for it now.

My ex-boyfriend and ex-best friend had taken the guest bedroom while my parents stayed in the master bedroom upstairs. My sister had her room across the hall from mine, and it worked. It meant I could somewhat have my own space from the two people who had betrayed me the most—something that annoyingly still hurt to think about. I couldn't wait for the day I felt nothing when I looked at them together.

I inhaled the crisp air, and I almost missed the scent of citronella candles that burned on this deck before the apocalypse. After the infection spread, insects and arachnids had disappeared.

No mosquitos, no spiders, no bugs at all.

While I loved the idea of a world with no bugs, it was unsettling.

We didn't know much about what caused it or how it spread so fast—just what the news outlets reported before they shut down. There were many different theories of what it was, but the main consensus was a virus.

I moved around the fire pit, careful not to trip over the pile of firewood next to it, and went down the stairs and onto the grass. The wide open pasture went on for miles both ways, and we used to let the livestock out to graze before we lost one of our cows to a zombie. Dad shot the cow and the zombie as soon as it happened. Our wooden fence around the perimeter of the land did a good job keeping out the wayward zombies, but the cow had strayed too far.

Other than that, it was quiet. We lived in the middle of nowhere, and it was a good thing we did since society collapsed.

I frowned and picked up my pace toward the weathered chicken coop, stepping over the chicken wire before unlatching and opening the narrow door.

Clucks and fluffs greeted me as I stepped in. "Good morning, ladies!"

The rooster shrieked, flapping his wings as he flew from a top spot of the coop.

I scoffed. "Oh, I'm sorry, Randy. Good morning to you, too. Spence will be in soon to feed you."

My sister, Spencer, handled feeding the chickens any scraps and garden leftovers while I collected the eggs.

We all had a job, and it made life after the apocalypse run smoothly.

I grabbed the small bin and gathered about fifteen or so eggs before turning around and catching a glimpse of someone in the doorway of the coop.

My heart slammed hard against my rib cage as I slapped my palm to my chest with a gasp. "Jesus, Mom, a little warning, please?"

Mom smiled, her gray bob moving back and forth as she shook her head. "Sorry, dear. I didn't mean to startle you. I was just checking in. I saw you wander out here."

"I'm fine. Just wanted to get an early start." I shrugged, leaving the coop as she latched it behind us.

"Tori, we've isolated from the start of the apocalypse. We haven't had outside contact since the internet went out." She pursed her lips, her light blue eyes that I inherited narrowing at me. "I know it's lonely."

I bit down on my bottom lip and nodded. "It is, but we're safe. Besides, we technically had the radio for the first year and a half."

She cocked her hip and rested her hand on it. "It went silent after six months, aside from the random warnings of hordes a year ago. All I'm saying is that you're twenty-six. I know this must be difficult, and I want you to know I'm here for you if you need to talk."

A pang of loneliness shot through my chest as I plastered on a reassuring smile. "Thanks, Mom. I'll let you know."

Letting out a sigh, she nodded. "I love you, Tori. I'm sorry it had to be this way. I couldn't have imagined you or Spencer would have to go through this."

Sadness weighed in my gut. I hated that she felt

guilty for bringing us into a world that ended in our lifetime. She and Dad had both bounced around the subject, but it was obvious to both me and Spencer that they felt responsible for us having to live in a post-apocalyptic world.

I balanced the metal bin on my hip and gave her a side hug. "I know, but we love you and Dad. We're so thankful for you guys."

"Listen, about Daisy and Jay…"

"I'm coping, Mom. *Really*. The fact that they're together doesn't bother me anymore. I mean, it did when it happened, but I've come to terms with that. What upsets me more is that I probably won't find anyone now. I mean, dating was hard before. In the apocalypse? It's totally hopeless. I mean, there are more dead men walking around than live. I just don't want to dwell on it."

She hugged me back tightly before pulling back. "Your dad said he'd be in the barn if you wanted to help milk the cows this morning."

"Okay. Thanks."

We walked back to the farm house, and a sigh of relief escaped me at the sight of an empty kitchen.

Mom gave me an understanding glance before smiling at me. "I'll go wash up and meet you in the barn."

"Okay." I placed the new eggs into the larger bin on the countertop near the fridge with a sigh.

Surviving had become routine. Nothing really exciting happened anymore. It made me wonder what other survivors were doing and where they were.

I would be lying if I said I wasn't curious about the state of the world outside of our bubble, but I also knew we were safe here.

"Need help with anything?" Jay's voice startled me as I whipped around to face him.

He leaned against the fridge with his arms crossed over his chest. Dirty brown locks fell into his eyes as he studied me cautiously.

My heart dropped to my gut.

The man hadn't spoken to me one-on-one for three entire years. Neither he nor Daisy had apologized to me for their actions.

My brows furrowed together as I shook my head. "Just clean the coop and barn today like usual."

"Got it." He stared at me long enough for my skin to crawl under his gaze. "We just want to make sure we're doing our part."

"Sure are."

"Seriously, Tor, you and your parents didn't have to take us in. We really *do* appreciate it."

I stiffened at the old nickname both he and Daisy used to call me. "Please don't call me that. You are both doing your part by keeping the animals' space clean and helping with harvesting food when needed. Why are you talking to me anyway?"

He let out a long sigh. "Daisy and I were talking last night, and to be honest, she misses you."

"She *misses me?*" A sarcastic laugh bubbled in my throat, and the years of resentment scorched my veins. "She was my best friend, Jay. Surely you both knew well enough that if you were fucking each other behind my back there wasn't any going back from that. For either of you. *Especially* the way I found out."

"Seriously?" Daisy scoffed as she came into the kitchen, running a hand through her straight blonde hair. "It's been years, and we're living in the apocalypse. Sure, we messed up. We went about our relationship the wrong way, but oh my God, Tor. We've done everything we can to make it up to you, but all you do is pretend we don't exist."

Wiping my clammy palms on my leggings, I cleared my throat and moved past Jay toward the door. "You two haven't attempted to speak to me like this until now, and to be honest, that's how I prefer it. If you miss me, that's probably just a guilty conscience. Even if I did miss our friendship, I don't want anything to do with it now."

"Tor, wait-" Jay started, but I hurried out of the house before I could hear anything else, the screen door slamming shut behind me.

My heartbeat pounded deafeningly loud in my

skull as I forced my legs to keep me upright as I strode toward the big red barn.

Jay and Daisy used to be the two most important people in my life at one time. I didn't understand how they expected me to get over the fact that they'd been seeing each other behind my back for who knew how long before I found out.

For the most part, I *was* over it.

But even so, I didn't want to befriend either of them again—and I shouldn't have to.

The earthy and dusty scent of the barn filled my nose as I stepped inside. "Dad?"

"Over here, honeybee! Just finishing up with ole' Bessie here. I woke up earlier than usual, so she's the last one." Dad peeked out from behind our oldest cow with a bright smile on his face. His red hair had patches of white throughout it due to age, and it was probably the coolest hair ever.

Spencer ended up with Dad's red hair, while I had Mom's brown, but I had Mom's blue eyes, and she had Dad's brown eyes.

I grabbed the milk bucket from him before placing it in the refrigerator we had in the barn. I was more than thankful we had the refrigerator, thanks to the wind and solar power from our ranch.

"Okay, so why the hell did Jay and Daisy try to corner you in the kitchen?" Spencer walked into the barn, her voice echoing from the rafters.

"They did what?" Dad asked gruffly as he rose to his feet and patted Bessie.

I groaned, slapping my hand over my face before facing them. "Jay offered to help out more on the ranch, which was weird, but then Daisy came in. She basically told me to get over what happened in the past because she apparently missed me."

Dad's frown deepened, but before he could no doubt bad mouth them, Spencer did it for him.

"I don't know why you didn't just leave them on their own when shit went down. I would've left them for zombie food. Plus, Daisy's a bitch around here to you and me—even if she does help out." Spencer rolled her eyes before sighing dramatically.

"Spence," Dad scolded her without much heat behind his words. "We can't *say* that."

"You think it all you want. I'll say it," she grumbled.

"I wonder that at times," I admitted, scrunching up my nose. "But I don't like that side of myself. Too bloodthirsty. Besides, all I did was bash zombie skulls to get to the car and the two of them joined. Jay actually saved me from being bitten. If he wasn't there, I wouldn't be here now."

The atmosphere grew heavy as I explained the real reason they'd tagged along. I had told Spencer what had happened with Jay and Daisy, but I hadn't ever gone into detail about how we'd taken on the zombies to make it home in the first place. It wasn't something I liked to think about.

Dad let out a ragged breath before running a hand through his hair. "Well. I never liked the kid, but I guess he's not the *worst* person if he saved my baby girl."

"I still hate them." Spencer pouted as we started to lock up the barn.

"I don't blame you," I murmured.

Daisy had practically grown up alongside Spencer and I. Her parents used to be really close with my parents, but they had never found their way to the ranch. Daisy had assumed the worst, but she had Jay to comfort her.

Spencer was just as shocked as I was about their betrayal.

Dad latched the lock on the barn door before I heard shouts on the wind, making my spine snap straight.

The three of us whirled around to see two men running through the pastures, waving their arms wildly around as they shouted something at us.

"Spencer, go tell everyone to stay inside and lock the doors, *now*," Dad stated gravely, and she took off without hesitation toward the house.

"I'm not leaving you alone with them," I said stubbornly, swallowing a lump in my throat.

"I figured." He stalked closer toward the pasture with me at his side.

The closer the men got, the more my nerves grew.

"What's your business here?" Dad barked at them as they stopped running and ambled toward us the rest of the way until we were a few feet apart.

The man who spoke first had shoulder-length brown hair with a beard, and he had tattoos on his arms, slightly obscured by his rolled up flannel sleeves. An axe was gripped in his hand, and a longbow was slung over his back with a quiver of arrows. His eyes were a beautiful honey brown that made me want to melt when his gaze snagged on me.

"There's a *massive* horde coming this way. We were scavenging in the city when we saw it heading through. We've outrun it for a few days, but the horde is larger than any I've seen before," he explained, his chest rising and falling rapidly as he caught his breath.

"This place you got here won't outlast it," the other said with a wince.

Logical thinking went out the window as I stared at him.

He was just as attractive as his friend, but in a different way. With blond messy hair, blue eyes, and a soul patch on his chin, he was utterly handsome. He had a rifle strapped to his backpack and a handgun on his waist.

They were capable of surviving out there in the

apocalypse, which made them dangerous. I knew that, but I entertained the idea of them staying with us. Which was silly. It had been far too long since I'd seen anyone outside our circle, and my loneliness clearly messed with my judgment.

"We have a cellar we can wait it out in," Dad stated, eying the two as he stepped protectively in front of me.

"Is the cellar protected with a secure latch somewhere hidden?" The blond rose a brow.

Dad hesitated, and I shook my head as I answered, "It's an outside opening."

"With all due respect, a cellar underground with only one exit ain't that safe," the brunette eluded, glancing back over his shoulder before focusing on us again. "Largest horde I've ever seen, and I've seen a couple since the world went to shit. It'll take at least a few days to pass through, and they could easily break into a cellar if they know you're there."

The two shared a brief look before the blond sighed. "It's up to you, but you're welcome to come with us. We have a type of oasis set up with a few other survivors. Safe enough to wait out the horde. You're welcome to come back after it passes if you want. Up to you though. We've wasted enough time as it is. The horde's only a couple of hours behind us. We need to go. There's not much time for you to decide."

"Dad…" My voice cracked as I looked toward

him, something in my gut urging me to listen to them. "Maybe we should go."

My family had taught me from a young age that intuition never steered me wrong, something I wished I had listened to regarding the feelings I had when the affair happened. I *knew* something was wrong but didn't listen. I vowed to always listen to my gut after, and my gut told me we should go with them.

From the grim look on Dad's face—his gut told him the same thing.

"We'll have to get the others," Dad stated. "And secure the ranch best we can."

"How many others?" the blond asked.

"Four besides us," I said.

"You have five minutes." The brunette glanced over his shoulder again. "Then we're leaving. With or without you."

"Got it." Dad grabbed my hand and pulled me away from the two men before I came to my senses and went toward the house.

"Oh God." My stomach dropped. "What about the animals?"

"We'll lock up best we can. Take the horses with us."

I nodded, my chest aching at the thought of leaving our chickens, rooster, cows, and bull alone to fend off the zombies.

As soon as we stepped on the porch, Mom,

Spencer, Jay, and Daisy filed out, eyes trained on the two men by the barn.

"What do they want?" Mom asked warily.

"They're running from a horde. The kind they used to warn us about on the radio a year ago. The horde's coming this way, and they said they have a safe place to wait it out," Dad shortened the explanation.

"Sounds like a trap," Jay said, suspiciously glancing at the men.

"Why would we leave? We've never even seen a horde living here. Plus, the house should be safe enough," Daisy added, biting her lip. "Right?"

"There's urgency and sincerity in their disposition." Dad shrugged. "I don't like the idea of leaving our home. But we gotta trust our guts on this one. Waiting this horde out doesn't sound like a good idea, and we have an opportunity not to."

"I trust your judgment," Mom said immediately as she wrapped an arm around his waist.

"Me too," Spencer declared.

"What do you think?" Jay asked, gaze directed at me.

I shifted on my feet, and one of the planks on the porch creaked. "I agree with Dad. They were urgent and warned us about an incoming threat. They could've just gone on their way, but they didn't."

Jay nodded, but Daisy frowned.

"Did you decide what you're going to do?" A gruff voice jolted our attention toward the guys standing at the base of the porch steps.

"We're coming. Just need to secure the place," Dad told them.

The brunette nodded, his warm gaze shifting over the group before landing on me. "I'm Micah."

"Nathan." The blond didn't even bother looking at the group as he winked toward me. "We'd be happy to help you lock up. We can't spend more than ten minutes at most. Then we *have* to leave."

"Gather any supplies you can. Food and water would be top priority," Micah added.

"Thanks." Mom smiled, oddly at ease as I was with the strangers. "I'm Grace."

"I'm Tom." Dad reached a hand out and shook theirs.

"Tori." I shook their hands, and Spencer introduced herself as she did the same.

"Why are you helping us?" Jay's jaw tightened, not offering them his name.

"Congratulations on using your brain." Nathan chuckled. "Most people these days will kill you without batting an eye, but we're not doing this for anything but good karma and extra hands for the Oasis we call home."

"We can come back if we want, right?" Daisy

asked timidly as Jay wrapped an arm around her and pulled her close.

"Of course. We're not kidnapping you." Micah ran a hand through his hair. "Gather everything you need. We need to be moving."

Twenty minutes later, the ranch was secured tight, and the animals had food to last them the week while we were gone.

Anxiety and dread coiled tight in my gut at the thought of a horde of zombies running through, but I hoped that our fence would maybe deter it if we were lucky.

We had gone this long without a horde breaking in after all.

"He's a beauty." Micah's gruff voice skittered down my spine as I finished cinching the saddle on Kovu and turned toward him.

"Thanks. He's my best friend." I smiled, heart swelling as I stroked my horse's neck. "He was born the same year I was, so he's always been there for me."

Kovu neighed like he was thanking him.

"How old are you?"

"Twenty-six." I smiled softly. "A horse's life-span

is usually around thirty years, so Kovu's pretty much an elder."

Kovu was a Rocky Mountain horse, and he was stunning. He had a sleek black coat with a light brown mane and tail. His looks only got better with age, and he was in great shape.

I made sure to take him on rides every single day—weather permitting.

A smile formed on my lips as I watched the man hold his hand out for Kovu to sniff before petting his head. "I think he likes you."

"That's good." His chuckle was deep and raspy, and it sent an excited chill through me. "I don't know much about horses."

"I could teach you some stuff if you want."

"I'd like that, darlin'," he confirmed, and my brain turned to mush at the cute name he'd said without much thought as he stroked my horse's head.

I stepped closer to him as I admired the golden flecks in his eyes. "So, Micah, what's your story?"

His lips curled into a smirk as he let his hand fall from Kovu, those pretty eyes of his trained on me. "Not much of a story to tell I'm afraid."

"I'll be the judge of that," I teased and stepped back, making sure all the carriers were fastened on the saddle bag. "How old are you?"

"Thirty-four." He gave a non-committable shrug.

I bit my lip. "That's an eight year difference between us then."

He barked out a raspy laugh. "It's the apocalypse. What does a little age difference hurt?"

His laughter made my chest warm, and my cheeks heated as I grinned. "Good point. Where exactly are you taking us?"

"The Oasis," he murmured, and I found myself loving the huskiness of his voice. I could've listened to him talk for ages, which was funny since he didn't seem like the type who talked much at all. "It's what we call our home. We live in the forest in what's kind of like a village of treehouses. I actually lived there before the apocalypse. It was just me then."

"Just you?"

A dark expression crossed his face as he nodded. "Just me."

"And who lives there with you now?"

The tightness in his expression faded. "Nathan and Calix live in my treehouse with me. We have a throuple who live in another, and then we have Nathan's dad and step-mom in the other. There's another treehouse we recently built as a type of guest space in case we find more survivors."

"That's really amazing," I said softly. "Does being up high really help with the zombies?"

He nodded. "They don't notice us. When and if they do, we just stay quiet and turn off any light in the house. They move on after a bit. We have pegs in the side of the tree as a make-shift ladder. Makes it highly unlikely they can get up."

"That's smart." A chill zipped down my spine as I thought of zombies being so close to where we slept and lived. At the ranch, I knew zombies were out there, but they *never* got close to the house.

The rest of the group made their way toward us, leading their horses with leather reins as they talked amongst themselves.

We had four horses on the ranch. It used to be five, but we lost Kovu's dad a few years before the apocalypse.

"We're ready when you are," Dad said as Mom fussed over their horse.

"Here's your bag." Spencer handed me my emergency satchel and golf club I had pre-packed in case of anything similar to this happening. I never expected to need it.

"Thanks, Spence."

"Grace and I will take Dolly. Tori and Spence will ride Kovu, Jay and Daisy will take Belle, and Micah and Nathan will ride Trigger," Dad said as Nathan cooed at Trigger like he was a dog and not a horse—not that Trigger seemed to mind.

"Thanks." Micah nodded as he shot me a comforting smile. "We'll come back after the horde passes and see what survives."

My gut rolled as a chilly breeze swept through, the long grass of the pasture shushing softly.

Nathan cleared his throat, and his blue eyes hardened. "Make sure any open wounds you have are covered, and if we encounter any infected—don't get their fluids in your eyes or mouth."

"Um, guys…" Spence uttered, her face paling before we looked in the direction she was staring at in horror.

The blood froze in my veins as I saw what was over the horizon.

Our pasture was mostly flat, so we could always see a far distance away—but nothing had ever elicited the gut-wrenching fear of what I saw in that moment.

A *massive*, shambling horde of zombies with no end to it appeared. It was far enough away that it was no wonder we hadn't noticed it before, but it was close enough to have us kicking our asses in gear.

"Let's get out of here," Micah grumbled. "It only looks about an hour or two from us."

Somehow, that didn't make me feel any better.

2

TORI

Queasiness lingered like a lead ball in my gut hours after we'd left home.

The horses kept a steady pace the entire time, as if they knew we were escaping some impending doom. Even Kovu, who had muscle spasms every now and then from going long distances.

My muscles ached, and my butt had gone numb from the ride. We hadn't ridden the horses for such a long period of time since we went into lockdown at the ranch. We hadn't even left our property since the day this whole thing started. I kept looking over my shoulder and scanning the area the best I could.

Nathan insisted that we didn't want to take any roads, and we believed him. I remembered the chaos when it all started. Driving through zombies and wrecked cars was something I'd tried to block from my memory, but it was no use. I remembered it vividly. The roads must've been in complete disarray even now.

The scenery changed back and forth between wooded areas and pastures, but the air turned even cooler as the sun left the high point in the sky. It didn't stop the sweat that coated my skin from the long ride though, and the farther we went, the less flat the land became. The horses were starting to tire from the rolling hills on our path.

I'd been surprised that Kovu hadn't insisted on a break yet, and he was having no trouble carrying both Spencer and me.

The sun dipped slightly below the horizon, making the sky alight with purples and blues that bathed the pasture.

"Nathan's cute," Spencer whispered in my ear, and I stiffened. "And he's *super* into you…"

"What do you mean?" I whipped my head toward her, and she giggled. "I haven't really spoken to him."

"He asked about you when we were saddling my horse. I mean, he was asking about everyone, but he asked me if you were seeing anyone in particular. The man definitely is attracted to you, and he is so sweet and funny. I'm telling you, Tori, *go for it.*"

"Really?" I looked to the front where Micah and Nathan rode ahead with my parents beside them. For not knowing much about horses, Micah learned how to ride quickly. "He *is* cute…but so is Micah."

"Micah too, huh? Well, we are in the apocalypse. *Why choose?*" She giggled.

"Spence," I hissed out.

"What? I'm just saying…if you like both of them and they like you, why not try it?"

"They probably wouldn't like that," I reasoned with her. "I mean, I don't even know if Micah is interested."

"How would you know? Did you ask?"

"I don't even *know* them!"

"You know they're hot."

"Spence-"

"*Tori*, come on! Live a little. You've been burned before. Why not just have a little fun and take this opportunity to move on from the past?"

I rolled my bottom lip into my mouth and bit it. She had a point. I didn't think I would even have a chance at finding anything romantic after the world ended. This *was* an opportunity for me to get to know them.

"Can we take a break? This ride is *killing* me!" Daisy groaned, her words muffled as she shoved her face against Jay's back.

"If we take a break, we will be increasing our risk of *actually* dying," Nathan said stiffly.

"But we just-" Daisy lifted her head before

cutting herself off with a high-pitch scream. "*Zombies!*"

Moans and strangled cries left the ghostly mouths of the small horde blocking our path as we came around the curved track.

My throat seized as I held back a scream of my own from the sight of them.

All the zombies I'd seen up until now had been clearly dead, rotten flesh and pitted skin. But the state of the more decomposed zombies that stood in our path was something out of an alien horror film. Human bones with mangled tendons and muscle hung off as they dragged themselves forward. Their teeth were rotten as they snapped their jaws at the air.

Nathan and Micah dismounted their horse without any hesitation, and Nathan brought his rifle up and shot through the skulls of a couple of zombies. The sound wasn't anything like the guns my parents had. It was quieter, which was a pleasant surprise.

Micah rushed forward, slamming his axe into the head of one zombie before turning and hitting another.

They took out the zombies seamlessly, like a team. It made me wonder just how many times they'd done it before.

Nathan moved forward, rifle up on his shoulder as he scoped the area. The sounds of their boots crunching as they walked over the disposed dead and cleared the area was sickening.

Micah was just ahead of Nathan, and neither of them saw the blood-caked fingers digging into the soil and pulling its upper body out from the high grass next to Nathan.

Adrenaline slammed into me as I jumped off Kovu, grabbing the golf club that had been secured to the saddle bag.

"Tori! What're you doing?" Mom gasped, and the rest of their shouts blended together as I raced toward Nathan just as the zombie's hand curled around his ankle.

Nathan's head snapped down as horror enveloped his features.

I swung the club over my head and struck down on the back of the zombie's head with as much force as I could muster.

The crack of the skull came easier than any I'd killed before, and brain matter splattered everywhere. Sounds of puking erupted from behind us, and I swallowed the burning bile in my throat as I stumbled back with my golf club clenched in my hand.

"Fuck. Nathan, I'm sorry." Micah rushed back to us, checking both of us over with his eyes. "I didn't check the high grass enough."

"Don't be. You did your job. That was on me. If it wasn't for Tori, though…"

"Good arm on you, darlin'," Micah finished, nodding at me with relief clear on his face.

"Darlin'?" Nathan forced out a breathy chuckle, the color in his cheeks starting to return. "I think killer is more appropriate. Thanks for saving my life, *killer*."

"Anytime," I replied, forcing my lungs to inflate and deflate with oxygen as my heart pounded mercilessly in my chest.

"You need something better than a golf club," Micah stated, his lips thinning into a grim line.

"No. I like my golf club," I defended as I adjusted my grip on it. "It's light-weight and pretty brutal."

"You never liked my golf clubs before," Jay grumbled as he helped Daisy off the horse behind us.

I glanced down at the mush of a zombie head that I had made and shrugged. "They weren't as fun as they are now."

Nathan barked a laugh. "She's got a damn good point."

"It's not like you used the golf club much through the years anyway," Daisy said as the rest of the group walked over. "Not after we made it to the ranch at least."

The horses kicked their hooves at the ground, refusing to come close to the dead.

"She's killed the majority of the zombies that

came up on the fence back home." Spencer snorted. "How many have you killed?"

"None," Dad answered for her. "Care if we take a quick rest without the bickering? Horses need a break."

Micah and Nathan shared a look before nodding.

"We can only chance a five minute rest," Micah said.

"Good enough for me."

We'd led the horses around the dead zombies on the ground and moved far enough away from the carnage to feel comfortable. Some of us stood while others sat on the ground, and my muscles cried in relief for the break.

Micah and Nathan sat on each side of me, and the warmth of their shoulders spread to mine.

"So, why the golf club, killer?" Nathan broke a stick before digging it into the ground and carving a line in the dirt.

The entire group seemed to shift as I let out a heavy sigh. "When the apocalypse started, I had stormed out of Jay's house into a massive horde so I went back in and grabbed the first thing I saw which happened to be the golf club. It worked. I took down a lot of zombies on the way to my car."

"Why were you storming out of Jay's house?" Micah raised a brow as he scratched his beard.

"Technically it was my house too," I murmured,

not really caring to elaborate. I didn't want to air my dirty baggage to the first men I'd been attracted to in who knew how long.

"Jay and Tor were together for two years. That's why they were living together," Daisy interrupted, and Jay coughed before shooting her a glare.

A tingle swept up the back of my neck and across my face as I wrapped my arms around my waist.

"Maybe there was a reason Tori didn't want to tell them," Spencer snapped at her. "It's not your business, but I guess you love putting your nose where it doesn't belong. She did storm out of the house that day because she found *you* where you didn't belong."

Daisy's lips curled into a scowl. "So sorry our love was greater than theirs."

"Greater?" Spencer snorted, and Dad nudged her with his elbow. "What? I don't think any great love story starts out by sleeping with your best friend's boyfriend behind her back."

My face heated as I dipped my chin down and stared at the carved line Nathan had dug into the dirt. He'd abandoned the stick next to it, and I felt that both men were tense beside me.

"I wasn't just sleeping with him! We wanted to be together!" Daisy's voice turned shrill. "We *were* together when she wasn't around!"

"This isn't the time or place for this discussion,"

Mom stated firmly, but Spencer wouldn't let it go—not that I blamed her.

"You say that like Tori was the other woman. She was the one dating and living with him!" Spencer threw her hands up with a loud groan. "*God, are you that stupid?*"

"It's not my fault Tori decided to be infertile and couldn't give Jay the family he wanted!"

My body flinched as if I'd been physically hit, and my blood ran cold.

Jay slapped his hand over her mouth before her eyes widened. "Stop talking, Daisy! You don't need to defend our actions. We went about it the wrong way, and you agreed with me that we did. Getting defensive isn't helping our situation."

She kept her mouth shut as he moved his hand, and a warm tear trickled down my cheek before I wiped it away roughly with the back of my hand.

"Tori," Spencer whispered, the regret thick in her voice.

"It's fine." My voice cracked, and I forced myself to look up. "I might be infertile, but at least I can't have a baby in a post-apocalyptic world."

3

NATHAN

Glancing around the group, I noticed no one in particular looked as shocked as I felt, not even Micah, who wore his cool façade like a mask.

Daisy and Jay had betrayed the sweetheart of a woman next to me in the worst possible way, and she still *saved* them?

I couldn't wrap my mind around being that selfless, but at the start of the apocalypse, I had been in a very public area at the beginning. Survival meant numbers when the world ended, and I assumed that was her thought as well.

But with the way that woman spoke, I didn't know why the family *kept* her around.

"Daisy, I know this has all been hard on you, but there is no excuse for your behavior," Grace, Tori's mother, scolded her.

Daisy didn't reply, she just put her head down.

I wrapped my arm around Tori's waist and helped her to her feet. "Don't worry, killer. You dodged a bullet with those two. Besides, not having to worry about birth control is a plus in my book."

"Excuse me." Tom coughed, and my face heated as I shot him a sheepish smile.

"Sorry, sir. I'm just saying."

"Thanks, Nathan. That's another plus to infertility in this world," Tori murmured.

"Break's over," Micah said in the deepest gruff voice I'd heard from him. I knew that whole thing had pissed him off just as bad as me.

Tori had to be the prettiest woman I'd ever laid my eyes on, and the way she held herself was magnetizing.

I led her back to her horse, reaching out and petting him. "Take good care of your owner." The horse puffed out air before nodding his large head, and I grinned. "You're a smart one."

"He really is," she murmured, glancing up at me briefly before turning back to the horse and kissing his forehead.

My heart seemed to stutter in my chest at the way her big blue eyes had stared up at me in the dark.

There was barely any light out as the sun dropped below the horizon and the crescent moon started to rise.

I glanced up toward the sky. The sunset had faded into twilight, and we still had a good few hours left until we made it back home. "Need help up?" I turned toward her, but she had already hauled herself up on the horse.

She let a slow smile spread over her lips as she shrugged. "I think I've got it...but thanks."

Spencer hopped up behind her sister and winked at me. "We got it, but Tori will definitely need your help later."

"Spence!" Tori's cheeks tinged with pink, and I sent her a large smile before winking and making my way toward Micah, who was already up on the horse.

I put my foot in the stirrup and moved myself up onto the saddle. The saddle was big, but I hated how it still managed to squish Micah and I together. I'd much rather have ridden bareback. My ass hurt.

"Did you have to flirt so openly at a time like that?" Micah asked once we were settled on the horse.

I shrugged. "I wanted to hit on her *and* comfort her. That's all."

"How much longer do we have?" Grace asked as the horses started to get into a rhythm toward our home.

"Few more hours, I'd say," Micah grumbled. "We have to keep going. If we stop, the horde will catch up, and I don't want to go out that way."

The group fell into silence again, and the farther we rode into the forest, the darker it was.

I was impressed the horses were doing so well.

"Fuck," Micah cursed as a branch whacked him in the head.

I stifled a laugh, and he grumbled something obscene under his breath at me.

"What are the treehouses like that you live in?" Tori asked, her voice stark against the quiet night.

"Micah's is the biggest," I told her. "Mainly because he built it before all this, but the layout is similar in each one."

"Two rooms, an area for the living room and kitchen area, and a bathroom with a toilet," Micah explained.

"What about a shower?" Spencer asked, and Micah chuckled.

"We have an outdoor shower. It's in a shed so you have privacy, but getting a shower set up was more difficult than you'd think. There's a sink in there, though."

"You'll all have to pile into the guest treehouse to ride out the horde," I added as the horse picked up its speed.

"Have you ever seen a horde before?" Jay asked, and I immediately recoiled at the sound of his voice.

How could Tori deal with someone like him?

How could he even bring himself to cheat on a woman like that?

Her infertility shouldn't fucking matter if he cared about her.

"Seen a few hordes run through," Micah bit out.

"We want to go home after this though," Grace said softly. "The ranch is our home."

"We appreciate you letting us ride the horde out in a safer place, but that is our home as my wife said," Tom clarified.

I scrunched my face up in a wince. They had not seen what a horde was capable of. That ranch had little chance of actually surviving it.

"We get that," Micah said.

"But the offer is always open," I added, specifically thinking of the cute brunette woman who had saved my life with a *golf club*. "My father's a prepper. He and I always joked about how the apocalypse would come about. I told him zombies, but his thought was society collapsing or nuclear war… I never thought I would be disappointed to be right."

"I get that," Tori spoke softly. "I played a lot of zombie video games before everything, and seeing it play out in real life is a lot less thrilling."

"Same here." My lips curved into a small smile.

We had a lot more in common than I suspected.

I hadn't been this interested in a woman since

the night my father, step-mother, and I lost our home.

Going down this road could've been dangerous, but my gut told me that Tori was safe.

Micah glanced over his shoulder back at the woman we had both become infatuated with before turning back to the front.

She could be the key to a type of happiness we had long given up trying to achieve.

4

MICAH

"Are we getting any closer?" Grace asked, exhaustion dripping from her voice.

The horses had slowed their trot to a walk, and the group had tired themselves out.

The crescent moon hung high in the sky accompanied by a billion twinkles of stars that lit the way. We'd passed almost completely through the pasture that led to the forest home of the Oasis.

"We're only an hour out now," Nathan answered. "We normally would've camped three nights from the city and one night from the distance of your ranch. We need to get back as soon as possible to warn the others of the incoming horde and prepare."

The group fell silent, matching the nightlife as we drew closer to the woods.

"The forest being this quiet used to mean there

was a large predator around." I gave a heavy sigh. The crunch of dead pine needles and twigs under the horses' hooves and our breaths filled the air, but nothing else. "But the roles have changed now. These days, the forest is indefinitely this quiet—unless there's something making noise."

"That's ominous," Tori murmured, and my chest tightened.

That woman made me feel things I hadn't since Kelly, and it didn't feel as unwanted as I thought it would. It made me want to *protect* her.

"I miss the ranch," Spencer whined.

"You've really lived in a bubble the last three years of this shit storm," I said. "Count your blessings. Things aren't so good out here. Stay alert."

The group didn't say anything else as we left the pasture and entered the forest.

This area was fully wooded, and it went on for *miles*. It was why I chose it to make my homestead. It was *far* away from people.

I had to use the four-wheeler to get to my truck next to the road if I ever wanted to go anywhere. Fuel had long run out though. Any motor-vehicles that relied solely on gasoline had become a thing of the past.

A branch snapped, and our horse jerked, causing the horses behind us to get spooked and try to run off. The rest of the group fought to get a handle on their horses as I narrowed my eyes toward the thick-rowed trees to our left and pulled back on the reins until the horse came to a stop.

Distinct moans echoed through the forest just before a zombie sprinted from the darkness with speed I had only witnessed in someone freshly turned. The moonlight filtered through the leaves above, showing that its muscles and body were still intact.

"Get the horses under control, and watch out!" I shouted, jumping off the horse as Nathan took the reins and tried calming it down.

All the horses reared up and bucked, distracting everyone else from the zombie that leapt forward and sank its teeth into the back leg of the first horse it could—Tori's horse.

My heart plummeted into my stomach, and the horse gave a bone-chilling groan as it went down, the zombie's teeth still embedded in its flesh. The horse must've already been at its limit because it didn't even try to run.

Tori and Spencer went down with it, but Tori fell to the side, rolling with the impact, while the horse fell on top of Spencer's leg with desperate groans.

"*Tori!*" Spencer's panicked voice was laced with pain as she pushed at the horse and tried scrambling out from under it.

I rushed toward them, weaving around the

chaos of the horses, but Tori moved faster than I did.

She pushed off the ground and raced back toward her sister and horse as the zombie yanked a chunk of flesh from the horse and spat it out on the ground as it found its next victim.

Zombies had one motive: to bite and infect.

They didn't eat like the mainstream media had eluded before the world ended.

The infected corpses didn't care about anything except spreading the soul-sucking virus as it crawled over the horse's struggling body, intent on getting to Spencer as she screamed for help.

I made it to them just as Tori threw herself over Spencer and kicked the zombie in the face to force it back, but the zombie's mouth chomped down, wrapping its fingers around her ankle.

My vision pulsed red with fury at Tori being at the mercy of a zombie.

An intense desire to protect her bloomed deep within me, and I lifted my axe over my shoulder, bringing it down onto the zombie's head before it could pull its teeth out of the rubber of Tori's sneakers and try to bite again.

The skull split with a crack before its jaw loosened, and it slumped forward.

"Oh my God," Tori whimpered, shaking her foot until the zombie fell off the horse to the ground.

Its teeth had been an inch or so deep into the thick rubber part of Tori's sneakers—just the sneakers.

Relief swept through me.

"Help me get her out from under him." Her voice cracked as she moved her arms under Spencer's and pulled.

"Of course, darlin'." My throat thickened as I bent down and lifted the horse up enough for Tori to free her sister's leg and laid the horse back down.

"Spencer, Tori, are you okay?" Grace's frantic tone sent a pang of remembrance of my mother before I pushed it away.

"We're fine," Spencer assured as she rubbed her leg and flicked her watery gaze toward the horse. "But Kovu's not."

"I've got Spence." Grace fussed over Spencer's leg as she helped her to her feet, and miraculously her leg wasn't broken. "She's fine, Tori. Go to him."

Saying that seemed to clear any of Tori's hesitation.

Her face crumbled as she turned and dropped back to her knees next to Kovu's head. She slipped the horse's large head into her lap and stroked his face as he groaned and squirmed in pain.

Tears dripped down her face and landed in small splatters on the horse's fur. "I'm so sorry, Kovu."

The horse blinked up at her, and while I didn't

know much about horses, it was clear that Kovu loved her just as much as she loved him.

"I'm so sorry I didn't see it." She gritted her teeth as the tears flowed freely. "I know it hurts."

"Tori…" Nathan stepped beside me, rifle perched on his shoulder as he kept checking the perimeter. He'd managed to tie the horse we'd ridden to a tree limb a few feet away, and it was huffing and pacing while trying to break free.

The havoc of the situation had startled everyone, including all the horses, and we had a newly turned zombie attack us from nowhere.

Adrenaline flooded me, which made slowing my heart rate down difficult.

"It's only a wound. We can make it past this. I just need something to use as a bandage." Tori sniffled, stroking the horse's face gently.

"He was bitten, Tori," I whispered.

"I know." Her lip wobbled as she stared over at the gaping hole at the top of the horse's leg. "But it's not that bad, right? We can get past this."

"The zombie was freshly turned which means there could be more newly turned zombies or some other survivors around. The area's not safe," Nathan added next to me.

"But he can still get up. He may be older, but he's a tank. Right, Kovu?" Tori stroked her horse's neck as he groaned. "Come on. Let's take that saddle off, and we can walk with you until we get there."

"Tori," I said again in a firm voice, and her head snapped toward me as tears slid down her pale cheeks.

"Why are you looking at me like that?" She shook her head slowly as she leaned over Kovu, shaking with every breath she took. "*No*. You can't mean to take him from me. It's just a bite!"

"He was bitten by a zombie. He's *infected*. He'll turn." I swallowed hard as disbelief contorted her expression.

"What do you mean he'll turn?" Tom asked as Daisy and Jay joined us. "He's a horse."

The horses were finally starting to calm down, snorting and neighing less.

"A bite is fatal," Nathan clarified gently. "The horse is as good as dead already. The virus is spreading through that horse right now. It's why he's in so much pain."

Tori shook her head back and forth, hair swishing around her as a whimpered cry left her throat. "Since when do animals turn?"

"The mutation didn't start until a year after the apocalypse. Around the same time the insects and arachnids died off," Nathan explained.

"Fuck!" Tori cried, her body shaking as sobs wracked her.

Watching her mourn her horse made my chest tighten to the point it was hard to breathe.

Her sister moved to her side and wrapped her arms around her. "Tori, we can't let him suffer."

"I know." Her voice cracked between sobs. "I know what we have to do, but *I don't want to*."

Daisy and Jay had enough sense to head back to their horse and give her the privacy she deserved.

"She can ride with us," Nathan whispered to Tom and Grace.

"Thank you." Grace's voice was thick with sadness. "We'll have Spencer ride with us."

"Goodbye, handsome," Spencer murmured as she pulled back from her sister and stroked the horse's neck lovingly.

Grace and Tom helped Spencer up before saying their goodbyes to Kovu and taking Spencer with them to get situated on the horse.

"Do you want to be the one to do it?" Nathan asked softly, concern shining in his gaze as he offered her his gun, but she shook her head.

"I don't think I can," she croaked, petting him.

"Do you want me to?" he offered, and she nodded her head as fat tears soaked her cheeks.

Echos of groans and moans flitted through the trees around us, and we straightened.

"Tori, I'm sorry, but we have to go right now," I told her, loud enough for everyone else to hear.

"I'm so sorry, Kovu. I love you so much." Tori

kissed her horse's forehead before gently laying his head back down on the ground. "You were the best horse ever, and I would never let you suffer."

The horse let out another rough groan before trying to nod its head at her, but that only made her sob harder.

"Make it quick, please," she requested before pressing another kiss to his head.

I held my hand out for her to grab and hauled her back up to her feet. Her grip on my hand tightened, and I didn't let go as she stood trembling beside me.

"I will," Nathan promised before aiming his gun at Kovu just as his eyes fell shut.

The gun went off, and Tori whipped her head into my chest as she jumped. She let go of my hand and wrapped her arms around my waist.

My throat thickened as I wrapped her in an embrace as she cried. "It'll be okay, darlin'."

Getting everything settled for the ride was a blur as I continued to hold Tori in my arms, and the sounds of the dead approaching became louder with every passing minute.

Nathan got the saddle bag off Kovu and gave it to Tom before he secured the golf club to his backpack with his rifle, and then he took our saddle off with Tom's help.

Daisy and Jay remained silent the entire time, but I could feel their eyes on her. The entire group had been worried about her and the approaching horde.

I scooped Tori into my arms, and she braced her hands on my chest. "I'm sorry."

"For what?"

"Losing it. I know it's a dangerous situation. I'm sorry."

"Don't worry, darlin'." I set her back on her feet next to the horse we were riding before hauling myself up on the horse's back.

She glanced back at Kovu before swallowing hard and getting up behind me before Nathan could offer to help.

Nathan got up with a groan behind her. "Move forward a bit."

I scooted up as far as I could, and Tori pressed close behind me, wrapping her arms around my waist. "Better?"

He sighed in relief. "Yeah, thanks."

My stomach churned at leaving Kovu's body in the forest without burying him, but we didn't have the time to waste. Not when the horde could be heard.

"Let's go," I stated. "We've stayed too long as it is. Stay alert. Who knows what could be in the woods with us now."

The horses were slower and more skittish than before as we went down the path in the forest toward the Oasis.

Tori had handled the situation logically, even if she'd been overwhelmed by grief. She'd saved her sister, and she'd tried to save Kovu.

There was nothing we could've done about the zombie. It had been newly turned, and it had caught everyone off guard. I needed to make sure she understood that once she came to terms with his death.

Her warmth surrounded me as she held onto me from behind, and her sobs mellowed into soft cries.

"I got you, killer," Nathan murmured, and I felt his arms brush my back as his arms circled her waist. "Relax."

Nathan was interested in her too, and that didn't surprise me. He'd always been one to wear his heart on his sleeve. I admired him for that, and it made me wonder how Calix would react to such a stunning woman when he met her, especially with his limitations.

Because after this, I didn't want to think of saying goodbye to her.

5

TORI

My chest felt like there was a jagged, gaping hole within it as we continued on the path to the Oasis, Kovu left behind with a zombie bite on his leg and a bullet in his skull.

He was a great horse, and we did everything together throughout the years. He tagged along with me for every chore I had at the ranch, and we rode the trails any chance we had. He'd been my best friend, and while I knew we did what had to be done, it *hurt*.

I appreciated Nathan making it so Kovu didn't suffer, and it was quick.

We hadn't known that animals were able to be infected from the virus, and that alone was dangerous. What other knowledge about the world did we lack?

"Anything we should know when we get there?" Dad asked, his tone solemn.

"We have a dog chained up and muzzled on the outskirts of the Oasis itself," Micah stated grimly. "He was turned the second year into the apocalypse, and I didn't have the heart to put him down the first couple of days. Sometimes I wish I had done it, but then we noticed the zombies avoided him and the area around him, so he is a good deterrent."

"My dog was killed by zombies too," Daisy piped up for the first time since Kovu was put down, and her voice made my skin crawl.

Nathan's arms tightened around my waist the same time mine tightened around Micah's, and a strange sensation spread through my body at being pressed between them.

I found them both attractive, but the feeling wasn't anything like arousal. It was more of a comforting feeling that made me feel *safe*.

Which was insane to me since I'd only known them for a few hours. Had the lack of outside contact turned me into someone who sought physical affection from others?

"I'm sorry to hear that," Nathan said, but his words didn't sound sincere.

It was a breath of fresh air to meet a couple of men who didn't fall for Daisy's innocent façade, and that only made me like them more.

"Daisy, you don't actually know what happened to Tiny," Jay reminded her, saying exactly what I had been thinking.

Daisy groaned. "Okay, I may not have actually seen it happen. But I assume that's what happened since she was in my apartment when everything happened. She was a chihuahua, so she didn't have many survival skills."

"That's fucked up," Nathan whispered, his hot breath fanning over the shell of my ear.

I buried my face against Micah's back to hold in a snort.

Daisy had always been selfish, but it was never that bad. She was my best friend for a reason. She used to come over every other day and have sleepovers with me—and they never stopped, even when I moved in with Jay. Though, now I understood that I wasn't the reason she had stayed by my side so long.

Once I caught her and Jay together, her personality went to shit—or maybe that was how she always was, and I had finally seen just how bad it was.

A familiar pang of loneliness shot through my chest as I thought about how I'd isolated myself when we got to the ranch after I'd caught them together. I spent more time with Kovu over the last three years than with Spencer, and I didn't even tell

Spencer what happened until a week after we'd made it home.

But Kovu knew, and he was my biggest comfort during that time…and now he was gone.

"Can you explain more about how it works at the Oasis?" Dad asked. "Like how you've been surviving there."

Nathan cleared his throat as he moved his head back to glance at my dad. "We're like a village. A series of treehouses in close proximity, and we have working toilets and a sink in each treehouse. Thanks to Micah and my dad having some plumbing knowledge, they were able to work with the pipes and make a pit latrine. It works. Plus, we have the shower shed outside for showers, and we bathe in the river sometimes."

"You have electricity, right?" Daisy's voice had taken on a whiney, irritable tone.

Micah and Nathan both snorted.

"We have candles for light, but those are getting limited. We weren't able to gather any in our supply run since the horde showed up," Nathan explained.

"I'm sorry, *what?*"

"It's the apocalypse," Micah grunted the words out, irritation flaring in his voice.

"But we've had electricity all these years!"

"Not everyone's as blessed as you all were," Nathan snapped. "Majority of the human population were turned, so electricity has been mostly wiped out in the real world."

"We were blessed," Mom interjected. "But we are also blessed that you two warned us of the horde. Electricity or not, we are going to have a safe place to stay. Be grateful, Daisy."

She let out a small gasp. "I'm sorry, Grace. You're right."

"It's okay," Jay murmured to her. "I know it's a tough change, but it's necessary."

"Yeah. I know. I'm sorry."

"She always like that?" Nathan whispered lowly in my ear, and a chill spread down my body.

Being between them had really started to get to me, but not in a bad way.

"She's actually not, but she doesn't handle stress well. Never has," I whispered back.

"Not handling stress can get you killed now. Being overwhelmed isn't an excuse any more," Micah said, low enough for the rest of the group not to hear.

I didn't know what to say next, so we fell into another long silence the rest of the way to the Oasis.

My eyelids kept drooping shut, and I was more than grateful for Nathan's sturdy hold on me as I leaned against Micah because without them, I wouldn't be able to keep myself upright.

They may have been strangers, but was it bad

that I felt more comfortable with them than during the two years I had been with Jay?

Feelings were subjective, sure, but it didn't *feel* like this was a bad thing.

A low, guttural growl echoed through the trees, and my body barely responded—exhaustion clouding my responsiveness.

"What was that?"

"That's Bane. He's the dog I told you about," Micah answered, and relief poured into my muscles as I relaxed between them again.

"We're here?" Spencer asked, and they both made small noises of agreement.

The horses moved their walk to a trot as we sped past the muzzled and chained zombie dog that growled at us.

"That should be impossible," Dad muttered. "All of this should be."

Nathan chuckled, his chest vibrating against my back. "You were really sheltered at that ranch, huh?"

"Everything happening in the world is impossible—virus or not. You can't convince me otherwise," Micah added.

Micah pulled on the reins, and Trigger came to a halt along with the rest of the horses, and another shot of grief spread through me when I remembered Kovu wasn't with us.

Swallowing the lump in my throat, I forced my head to move up off Micah's back and look around.

My gaze widened as I took in what the Oasis actually was, and a pleasant humming vibrated in my chest.

It was the middle of the night, and yet the area was bathed in slivers of moonlight. I'd assume the Oasis would be beautiful and lit up on a full moon rather than the crescent in the sky.

Thick pine trees held up four treehouses that rounded in a circle around the small clearing the horses stopped in, and the cool air skimmed through lazily.

The treehouses were *massive*. I mean, not like a large house but more like an apartment. They were much bigger than I imagined a treehouse to be, and they looked well maintained.

There was a small wooden shed in the clearing between two of the houses, and between the other two houses sat a larger wooden shed almost the size of our living room back at the ranch.

"Micah, Nathan," a male voice hissed through the night as a man with blonde hair and black framed glasses came walking up with a flashlight. "What's going on? Where'd you get the horses and extra hands? You're back three days early."

"Good to see you too, Dad," Nathan grumbled as he got off the horse and helped me down before Micah jumped off. "Long story short, there's a horde only about half an hour behind us—if that. We had to run back, but we ran across their farm and told them about the horde and offered them sanctuary with us to ride it out."

I reached up and stroked Trigger, ignoring the grief swirling in my chest as he blew air from his nostrils and nudged me with his nose.

Spencer walked up next to me and bumped my shoulder with hers.

"Thirty minutes?" Nathan's dad ran a hand down his face. "We'll have to warn the rest. We usually have procedures for new survivors, but since there's a horde coming, we have little time to talk about things."

"We appreciate the hospitality," Dad stated, walking over and holding his hand out to the man.

He shook Dad's hand firmly, and they shared a brief smile. "We have an empty treehouse your family can stay in. It's stocked with everything you need. We'll have to go over more after it passes, but someone will come get you when it does. I'm Benjamin. Welcome to the Oasis."

"I'm Tom. This is my wife, Grace." Dad wrapped an arm around Mom and glanced at my sister and me. "These are our daughters, Spencer and Tori. Daisy and Jay are… Well, they've been staying with us."

"Good to meet you."

Benjamin cleared his throat. "Hordes are

intense. I don't know if you've been through one, but we'll probably be stuck up in the treehouse for a few days before we can come out."

"No electricity or a shower for days?" Daisy muttered to Jay, and my restraint snapped like a rubber band.

I whirled around on my heels and glowered at her. "Are you kidding me, Daisy? They've gone out of their way to *save our lives*, and you still find a way to complain about it."

Her mouth fell open before she closed it and scowled. "Just because you don't care about personal hygiene doesn't mean—"

"I *do* care about personal hygiene, but I recognize that our lives are more important than going a few days without a shower! Why can't you ever see the bigger picture?" My voice raised before a louder moan echoed back, and then several moans started to be heard from the forest.

"Maybe you two shouldn't be trapped together in a treehouse," Nathan muttered.

"Tori, you're welcome to stay in our cabin with us," Micah offered.

"That's a great idea," Spencer answered.

"Couldn't agree more for once." Daisy huffed.

"Hey, now—" Dad started to protest, but I turned back to the two men offering me their cabin.

"I'd love to. Thank you."

Both of their faces relaxed, and they seemed

pleased that I took them up on their offer—which solidified the decision.

"Tori, they're two *men* you don't know," Dad stated the obvious.

I opened my mouth to defend my decision, but Nathan stepped forward with a gentle smile. "I understand that, sir. But your cabin is right next to ours so you'll be able to look out the window and see Tori whenever you want. She will be safe with us. I promise you."

Dad's scowl softened slightly, and Benjamin spoke before he could. "My son would never let harm come to anyone so long as he can prevent it."

"I don't like it." Dad pursed his lips before focusing on me and sighing. "But I get it. As long as you're sure, honeybee?"

"Yes, Dad. I feel safe with them as it is," I admitted. "I need time away from *everything* anyway."

Jay flinched as Daisy smirked with an eye roll, but they didn't respond.

"I handle keeping all the water clean, and all the treehouses have enough food and water to last a couple of weeks," Benjamin explained. "We'll have to go over rules after the horde passes for now, but just do not use the wood stove at night during the horde. If you must use it, do it during the day. Try not to bring any attention to yourselves as it passes through."

"What about the horses?" I asked as Trigger kicked at the ground.

"They'll have to go into the bigger shed. We don't have much in terms of what horses need, but there's enough we can throw together to help them survive the horde," Benjamin explained. "We can do that now before I show you all the treehouses."

"We'll show Tori the treehouse," Nathan said, and his dad nodded. "Everyone stay safe."

I turned to my parents and gave them a hug before doing the same for my sister. "Stay safe. I love you guys."

"We love you," Mom murmured. "You be safe."

"I'm sorry," Jay interjected, running a hand through his hair. "But isn't it a dumb idea to allow Tori to be locked up in a treehouse with two random men?"

Daisy shot daggers at him as I tilted my head.

"Three, actually," Nathan corrected, and Micah snorted.

Jay blinked at them before frowning. "That's not any better."

"It's better than having Daisy keep making passive aggressive comments at Tori," Spencer pointed out, sticking her tongue out at Daisy.

"I assure you, your daughter will be safe with them," Benjamin promised as the moans and groans of the undead grew closer, sending a sickly feeling down to my gut. "But we need to all be in the treehouses as soon as we can."

"I want to stay with them," I told my parents. "I'll be fine. Less drama is better at a time like this anyway."

"Stop making a scene. It's not that serious." Daisy rolled her eyes.

I bit my tongue and hugged my family once more before we helped everyone situate the horses in the shed, and then Nathan and Micah led me to their treehouse.

Thick wooden pegs came out the side of the tree and led up to the platform of the treehouse, and Nathan was the first to go up before offering me his hand.

My hands grasped the rough wooden pegs as I climbed up and took his hand for him to help me up. "Thanks."

"You're welcome, killer."

Micah came up behind us and placed his hand on my lower back. "Ready to see our place, darlin'?"

A strange thrill of excitement spread through me as I took in the treehouse in front of me. Maybe I shouldn't have taken them up on their offer, but I'd been stuck with Jay and Daisy for three years. I needed a break from it all, and my intuition told me these two were good men.

"Absolutely."

6

CALIX

A creaky floorboard and a feminine voice echoed through the wooden walls, making me jerk awake in bed.

"I can't tell you how much I appreciate you allowing me to stay with you," a woman expressed her appreciation.

"We couldn't let you be stuck in the guest treehouse with *Daisy*," Nathan assured her, and the way he said Daisy was as if the name itself burned him.

"Calix won't mind. Just make sure to keep everything clean and disinfected," Micah added in his low, gruff tone that seemed softer than I'd ever heard it in the two years I'd known the man.

Hauling myself out of bed, I ran a hand through my unruly tangled hair and groaned before snatching the cotton mask on the nightstand and tucking it carefully over my ears to cover my mouth and nose.

I could hear the hissing of disinfectant as I stumbled toward the exit and grabbed a freshly cleaned pair of rubber gloves on the dresser. I slid them on before opening the door and going out into the living room.

The small amount of moonlight streamed through the window enough to make out a beautiful woman standing between Micah and Nathan, worrying her bottom lip between her teeth. Brown hair tumbled down her shoulders in waves, and her pretty blue eyes widened as she noticed me.

"And this is Calix," Nathan introduced me with a dramatic arm wave my way, and Micah finished spraying her off before setting the disinfectant on the table.

Her lips curved into a shy smile as she wrapped her arms around her torso. "Hi. I'm Tori. I'm sorry for barging in."

Her voice was soft and sweet, different than I had originally thought when I had been woken up by it, and her smile made my chest tighten.

I tilted my head and scanned my eyes over her sweatshirt and leggings, blood splatter coated both. The guys had deposited their shoes and hers outside like usual, so her feet were covered by faded blue socks. "You'll need to clean up. The room's already contaminated. Got extra clothes?"

Her smile dropped as her brows scrunched together. "Excuse me?"

"She will," Nathan interrupted. "We all will. We know how you are, man."

"Then why haven't you done it correctly? How'd you find her?" I turned my gaze to Micah, and he gave a heavy sigh.

"There's a horde coming through. We ran across her family's ranch, and they came with us. It's her, her sister and parents, and two others. She doesn't get along well with the two others, and there was arguing. Figured it'd be best not to have conflict during the horde passing through."

"*Horde*? How far away until it comes through?" My brain was still foggy from sleep, but the news of a horde making its way through sent adrenaline pumping through me.

"Any time now. The horde was too close for comfort on the way here." Nathan shivered.

"Do you think it's smart to have a *stranger* stay with us for days on end while an army of undead shamble below us?" My tone came out flat, but my heart felt like it would beat out of my chest.

"I can go stay with my family instead. I don't want to be an inconvenience," she offered just before Bane let out a snarl and some low rumbles outside.

"It's too late for that," Micah grumbled, turning

and locking the multiple locks on the door to the treehouse.

Nathan strode toward the window and glanced out. "Everyone is settled in their treehouses, and the horses are locked up in the shed. Besides, Bane only makes that noise when he senses the dead."

"I'm sorry." Tori glanced down after her feet.

"Don't be," I grunted, my skin crawling the longer my gaze kept snagging on the bloodied clothes they all wore. "Nathan, are you sure she's safe?"

"What's that supposed to mean?" Nathan's lips flattened. "Of course she's safe."

"Your impressions aren't always good," I reminded him, and he winced.

"She's safe," Micah stated with a warning gaze. "I'm a good judge of character. I vouch for her."

"I'm sure I can get to the other treehouse before the horde makes it through," Tori snapped, then whirled on her heels, and headed for the door.

Micah blocked her path the same moment Nathan started walking into my personal space.

"Your room, now," he practically growled at me.

He'd got so close to me with the blood on his clothes that my stomach rolled. "Bathroom," I compromised.

I didn't want him in my room with his clothes like that.

Once we stepped inside and shut the door, he glowered at me. "What the fuck, Calix?"

"What?" I grumbled, crossing my arms and leaning against the wall that I'd disinfected earlier that morning.

"It's good to be paranoid and skeptical about people in the world now." He stood, careful not to rub his dirtiness anywhere. "But we saved Tori and her group of survivors. They didn't seek us out. That poor girl has been through enough without you giving her the cold shoulder."

"I wasn't giving her a cold shoulder."

He shot me a firm look, and my shoulders sagged.

"Okay, fine. I was. *But can you blame me?* She's covered in blood! And she's been who-knows-where. What if she's sick? We don't know what kind of germs she's been exposed to, Nathan!" My head spun with different scenarios, and my throat thickened. "She could have her *period* here! That's a bodily waste!"

"We have precautions. We use pads and tampons for injuries, so we have some in here in case of that. But it probably won't happen. If it does, we will handle it," he assured me. "Listen, I get it. I do. But she's going to follow all the rules we do. It's going to be fine. Wait until you get to know her more. She's respectful and sweet."

I narrowed my gaze at the way his eyes lit up

and lips curled upward as he spoke about her. "You're infatuated with her."

"I'm not *infatuated*. I just like her is all."

Rolling my eyes, I pushed off the wall. "Whatever. She's staying, I get it. But she has to follow *all* the precautions in place."

"And she will. We will go over all of it in the morning."

I flinched. "Clothes?"

He frowned. "We'll take care of it, but would it kill you to be a little more welcoming?"

"It might if she's carrying a disease or something," I shot back before we left the bathroom.

Relief flooded me at Micah and Tori's appearances, and my muscles relaxed a bit.

They'd both ditched their bloodied clothes on the deck outside, and I assumed they'd wiped down with the disinfectant solution and brown cloths we had set aside for blood. They appeared to be cleaned up even by my standards.

One of Micah's flannels draped over her body, and she'd tied her hair up out of her face, revealing just how stunning she was.

Micah had gone through the routine for cleaning and disinfecting himself, but after I'd assured that, my eyes just stayed glued on her.

She shifted on her bare feet as she stared back at me. "I am sorry that I came uninvited."

"You were invited," Micah growled out,

frowning at me. "He just hasn't had a guest in our home before."

"Not even Benjamin?" she asked.

"Not even my dad," Nathan confirmed. "Calix is a germaphobe."

"Not *completely*." I cleared my throat, my cheeks burning as I called attention to myself. "I'm sorry for the hostile welcome. I just have to have things a certain way or it makes me anxious."

"I can imagine," she murmured, empathy shining in her eyes. "I'm sorry the world is the way it is. I can't imagine the anxiety you deal with daily. I'll do everything I can to make you comfortable with me being here."

My mouth fell open, and heat streaked through me. I'd never had anyone be so open to making adjustments to suit my needs—aside from Micah and Nathan.

My chest fluttered at her kindness. "Thank you, Tori. It's incredibly appreciated."

She smiled hesitantly before holding out her dainty hand, but I winced.

Even with her smooth clean skin, a pit formed in my gut at the germs she could possibly have crawling on her.

She jerked her hand back to her side a moment later. "I'm so sorry. I didn't think."

"It's fine," I croaked, stumbling back a few steps. "Where are we going to have her sleep?"

"I usually sleep on the couch," Nathan admitted to her as he went over and pulled out the worn leather pull-out sofa until a full-size bed took its place. He grabbed the pillow and a couple of blankets from the wicker basket beside it and threw them over the mattress. "But you're more than welcome to sleep with me."

"Or you can sleep in the bed with me," Micah offered as a smirk came over his features.

"Or Micah and Nathan could sleep together, and you could take the bed," I added the suggestion. "You know, in case the woman wanted the option of sleeping *alone*."

Both smirks on Micah and Nathan's face wiped off as concern replaced them.

"That's definitely an option." Micah scratched his beard.

"Yep. It is." Nathan cleared his throat. "Completely up to you, killer."

"How about I sleep on the couch, and you two can have the bed?" She gripped the edge of the flannel, which reached mid-thigh, and I swallowed hard.

"That's fine." Nathan shrugged.

"I don't mind if you want my bed," Micah offered again, but she shook her head.

"You've given me a safe place to stay. I'm not taking your bed. Besides, this is a nice pullout, and I am more than ready for sleep." She yawned, stretching her arms up over her head, and the flannel rose up.

Her skin looked *so soft.*

I turned my head before it went any further. "If you wouldn't mind disinfecting the toilet with spray and wipes every time you use the restroom, I would be in your debt."

"Of course," she replied easily, the pull-out squeaking as she crawled on top of it.

"Night," I murmured before turning and booking it out of the living room and to the safety of my room.

Once the door shut, I tore my mask off and peeled off the gloves before tossing them on the floor as I inhaled a deep breath.

I'd never *wanted* to physically *touch* another person before. I could handle Micah and Nathan if I knew they'd cleaned themselves right, but I'd never truly desired to *touch* someone.

Crawling back into my bed, I pulled the heavy comforter up and glanced at the door.

Tori would be sleeping just beyond that door for a few days, and it was abnormal just how much I didn't hate the idea.

7

TORI

This was a bad idea.

Guilt and regret swarmed in my gut as I stared at the closed door that Calix just walked into.

The man had been abrasive, and I hadn't expected him to be a germaphobe. It must've been an absolute nightmare for him to live in the world the way it was. Even though he'd worn a medical mask, his bright green eyes had been calculating and beautiful. His black hair had stuck up in every direction, and I felt bad for waking him. His voice had been deep, and it sent chills down my spine the more he talked.

I hated that I made him feel uncomfortable in his own home.

All because I hadn't wanted to deal with Daisy and Jay.

Micah cleared his throat and walked across the wooden floor to the kitchen area and waved his arm over the wooden cabinets and a wood stove. "It's getting chilly now that summer has ended, but with the horde, we don't want to start the wooden stove unless we're cooking something or it's below freezing."

Nathan strode toward an open door with a porcelain sink visible and jerked his thumb toward it. "This is the bathroom. When you're finished with your business, spray the disinfectant solution in the blue bottle and wipe it down with the blue cloth all over the toilet and bathroom for Calix's sake. For future reference, he has the cloths and spray bottles color-coded for each room. Blue is the bathroom, green is for the floors, white for walls, red for the kitchen, purple for the living room, and black for the bedrooms."

My face burned as I nodded, getting under the covers Nathan had laid out on the bed for me. "Sure. Thanks for letting me stay with you. I'm sorry I made Calix uncomfortable."

"You're welcome here. Calix will come around. Give him time." Nathan smiled, and my heart fluttered at how welcoming the two were—but I hated that I'd intruded on Calix's safe place.

"I don't know about you, but I'm beat." Micah yawned, stretching his arms over his head. His flannel rode up a bit to show his toned lower abdomen with a dark trail of hair leading into his pants. "Ready to get some sleep?"

I nodded. "If it wasn't for you, my family and I would've been terrified. I don't want to think of what would've happened had we seen the horde and had to deal with it on our own. *Thank you.*"

They both shot me reassuring smiles.

"Don't worry about it, killer. I'd be dead on my feet if it wasn't for you." Nathan gave me another longing look before retreating back into the door closest to the wood stove. "We'll leave the door open in case you need anything."

"We should really be thankin' you, darlin'," Micah said with a grin before following Nathan into his room.

My heart throbbed painfully in my chest as I snuggled down in the bed and let out a breath.

They were extremely kind. I hadn't met many people so open to helping others even before the apocalypse.

I hoped Spencer and my parents were doing okay in their treehouse. I didn't have time to think about the state of the world, our home, or even mourning Kovu because the moment my eyelids fluttered shut, exhaustion took over.

My body jerked awake, and the sheets and blankets stuck to the surface of my body.

Groans, moans, and shuffling came from below us, and fear leaked into me as I shot upright in bed with sweat rolling down my spine.

The moonlight still shone into the treehouse, but there was barely enough light to see, let alone move around in a place I didn't know well.

But my body screamed at me to get up anyway.

I tossed the covers off and slid out of the bed before tip-toeing over to the window.

My stomach rolled as I saw the amount of zombies making their way through the forest, miraculously not noticing us up in the treehouses. A shiver worked its way through me as horror knotted my gut.

An entire army of undead was below me.

If any of us had been down there, we would be dead. Just like that.

I hoped the horses were safe in the shed, but the way the horde came through made me think the worst. They destroyed everything in their path aside from the trees themselves.

The ranch wouldn't have survived this.

A tear slipped down my cheek, and I glanced up at the treehouse adjacent from ours to meet Jay's gaze.

He stood there, staring out the window same as

me, but his eyes were locked on me rather than the zombies.

You okay? he mouthed.

My brows furrowed for a moment.

Of course I wasn't okay. We'd all but lost our home and were forced to relocate with other survivors we knew nothing about.

But these survivors were kind, and they'd saved our lives.

I gave a stiff nod and turned before I shuffled toward Micah's room without another thought.

Jay didn't deserve to know anything about me anymore. Not after what he did. Jay hadn't just been my boyfriend, he had been my best friend along with Daisy.

Their betrayal hurt me deeper than I'd ever been hurt before.

I didn't want anything to do with them aside from surviving together, and I didn't see why I should have to waste energy speaking with them anymore than I had to.

The floorboard creaked at the threshold of the room, and Nathan shifted up in bed, holding his arm out to me. "Come to bed, killer."

"Did I wake you?"

"I've been up. Figured you'd need someone. I was terrified the first time a horde came through here too. Micah's so used to it, he can sleep through it now."

I reached out and took his hand. "Thank you, Nathan."

"Any time," he mumbled, pulling me over him and into the soft bed between him and Micah, curling his arm around me.

I stared at Micah's sleeping form next to me. "Are you sure Micah won't mind if I stayed in his bed with you both?"

"Not at all." His warmth consumed me, and I snuggled closer to him. "He'll just be happy you're comfortable."

"I hope so." I glanced up at him, but the moonlight was even more scarce in this room than the living room. "How many hordes have been through since you've been here?"

"Every year around this time actually, so two."

"You've been with Micah for two years then?"

He let out a ragged sigh before his fingers began to skim over my scalp, and I laid my head against the pillow. "Yeah. I fucked up really bad that first year, and that fuck up led to my dad, my step-mom, and me to flee our fortress of a homestead. After we fled, we were staying in a warehouse for a couple of months, and Micah came through to scavenge. That's how we met him, and when he learned our story, he offered us refuge here so long as we did our part."

"I'm sure whatever you did wasn't that bad," I murmured, my eyelids becoming heavier. "Besides, it led you to where you are now with Micah and Calix. It seems like you have a great set up here."

"That's one way to look at it. But you don't know what I did. That's a story for another day, though." He pulled me even closer. "Get some sleep, killer. You need it."

"I know." I slid my hands up his chest and slung one arm around his waist as if I'd been cuddling him forever. "You feel nice."

"So do you. Tell me if you get uncomfortable," he murmured.

"I won't, but you tell me the same."

"Having you in my arms is the most comfort I've felt in years."

I inhaled his spicy scent as I snuggled closer.

Sleep didn't take long to consume me again, and it was the best sleep I'd had in years.

8
MICAH

A faint scent of strawberries filled my nose as I inhaled deeply, and my eyes opened to Tori tucked between Nathan and me—both our arms snug around her waist. My flannel hung loose on her, but she was still covered and looked beautiful. It had ridden up in the middle of the night, so I avoided looking down, but her skin was *so* soft.

Amusement tugged at my lips as I stared at her. Her face was free of worry as she snored with a sweet smile on her face. She must've gotten scared last night, and Nathan brought her to bed. I was glad she felt comfortable enough to get in bed with us. The ruckus from the horde outside seemed like white noise now. I'd gotten used to it after the first horde went through without issue.

My Rotten Love Life

Slipping my arm from around her waist, I took another breath before dragging myself out of bed.

It had been *so* long since I'd laid in bed next to a woman. Not since Kelly.

I swallowed the hard lump in my throat and turned to force myself out of the room.

I didn't like thinking about Kelly, but my heart ached at the thought of her even now. She deserved so much better than what she got in this world. The only bright side to her death was that she didn't have to see the shit show the world had become.

It wasn't that Tori reminded me of Kelly—it was the opposite really.

Kelly was soft and timid, she refused to kill a bug, and she despised showing emotion. From what I'd seen, Tori was harder, didn't hesitate to kill when it was needed, showed her emotions, and she was honest.

Yet something inside of me compared the two of them, and that wasn't fair of me to do to either woman.

Calix paced the length of the kitchen, socked feet making dull thumps against the wooden floor as the wood stove crackled. His black hair stuck up in every direction, and he moved his mask to cover his face completely when he noticed me.

"Making something?" I yawned as I stopped in the doorway of the bathroom.

"Soup," he replied. "Make sure you—"

"Wipe down the toilet. I know." I shut the door and finished my morning piss before disinfecting the toilet, wiping everything down, and washing my hands. Then I sprayed the sink and wiped it down before leaving the bathroom to find Calix still pacing.

I leaned against the wall next to the wood stove. The aroma of chicken noodle soup hit me, and my stomach growled.

We had plenty of canned soup and foods, but we were also running against the shelf life of them all. Canned foods were perfect for the winter months, but we managed to can our own food too. There was a field a few miles east that we planted crops in during the spring months and harvested as we could. Sally, Benjamin's wife, knew a lot about canning foods so she and Ava did that.

Jack, Charles, Nathan, Calix, and I also hunted as well as scavenging. Benjamin handled everything water—which meant purifying it, building and maintaining water filters, and making sure there was enough for drinking water and enough in the tanks for the sinks and toilets as well as the shower outside.

Ava, Jack, and Charles were the throuple in the Oasis, and I always admired the love they held for each other.

The Oasis was our community, and everyone played a part in keeping us going. I loved everything about it. I'd originally moved into the forest to get away from people, but I think I needed the interaction more than I'd thought. They saved me in ways I hadn't realized I needed saving—and that woman curled up in bed beside Nathan was going to save me again.

"I was surprised to wake up and find the pull-out couch still pulled out without our guest," Calix mumbled, pausing his pacing before ambling back to the soup and stirring it.

"She woke up in the middle of the night. I woke up to her between Nathan and me in bed." I smirked. "She probably woke up and got scared of the horde."

"Probably," he agreed with a wince. "The first time a horde came through, it freaked me out. The thought of their dead, walking, diseased-ridden carcasses below us…" His face paled before he shook his head of the thought.

"I see you put away the covers and pushed the couch back in." My gaze scanned over the living room, cleaner than it had been when we came in last night. "Thanks."

"The mess was getting to me." He shrugged before turning around in a whirl, and his eyes snagged on my bedroom. "What's her story?"

My brows rose in surprise. "You're actually interested in it?"

"She's living with us for a few days. Of course I

am." He blinked at me with a huff. "Besides, she's sweet. I feel sorta bad for being so harsh on her last night, but I don't like people coming into my space unannounced."

"I know, but that's our fault. Not hers." I frowned.

"I know." He sighed, pinching the mask over his nose tighter. "So who's Daisy and why is she keeping that woman from staying in a treehouse with her own family?"

I snorted, and he glared at me. "Sorry, but you picked up a lot for knowing so little about the situation. From what I can tell, Daisy is her ex-best-friend and Jay is her ex-boyfriend. She caught them sleeping together the day the apocalypse started, and they've had to survive together ever since."

His eyes widened before he turned back to the soup and stirred it. "Wow."

"Yeah. She's tough, though."

"How'd the ride here go? The dynamic between them really that bad?"

"It's tense," I confirmed, crossing my arms in a huff as I thought back to the confrontation Daisy and Tori had. "Daisy went off on Tori to start drama, and she mentioned some pretty personal things in Tori and Jay's relationship. I don't know the whole story there, but it's clear it's a sensitive subject. So Daisy isn't above hitting below the belt, so to speak."

"Then this Daisy's a mean girl."

"Seems so. The only thing I can say is she had enough sense not to speak to Tori much after her horse was bitten."

His shoulders stiffened, and his green eyes slid over to meet mine. "She lost her horse last night?"

"Nathan had to put him down before he turned. She didn't know the virus had spread to animals. None of them did. They were in a bubble on that ranch, Calix. A damn good bubble."

A beat of silence passed between us as he nodded. "Must've been nice to live in a bubble through all this."

"Yes and no. Now they have to face reality after that bubble has popped. Their ranch is going to be nothing after this horde comes through." I shook my head, thinking of the animals still in that barn and coop. "I've never seen a horde this size, and I don't want to think what would've happened to them had they stayed at the ranch."

My gut churned at the thought of them bunkered down in that cellar.

"Every year it gets bigger," he muttered bitterly. "I swear they migrate like birds."

"They do." I rubbed my beard with a groan.

Every year just as fall hits, they run through. And every year, it grows.

I assumed the zombies would decline in numbers due to decay, but instead, they were rising.

It didn't make any scientific sense, but it was happening regardless. It had to have something to do with the fact these zombies didn't eat. They only spread the virus through a bite then moved on. I didn't like to concern myself with the logic behind it like Nathan and Calix did.

"I was glad to see her in the bed with you two. I thought she tried to leave or something." He set the spoon down and began pacing again.

I flinched before trying to force my muscles to relax. "That would be a nightmare."

"No kidding." His dull steps filled the room like a lull, and I focused mostly on that sound. "We're going to have so much to do when this horde passes through. How many days do you think it'll take to rebuild this year?"

"Not as long as last year. Benjamin, Jack, and Charles reinforced the hell out of the sheds. I'd be surprised to see them torn down again, but you never know." I frowned, despising the groans that came from underneath and around us. "At least we have more survivors this time."

"Unless they don't decide to stay," he added, and my chest ached at the thought of Tori leaving.

I didn't even know her. It shouldn't have mattered to me that she may not be staying—but it did.

9

TORI

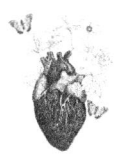

Comforting warmth surrounded me, distracting me from the moans and groans of the dead outside.

A heavy weight laid across my legs and torso, and I cracked my eyes open. Nathan's legs overlapped mine, and his arm was snug around my waist. The flannel Micah gave me to wear had slipped up, and I silently cursed myself for the comfortable white granny panties.

It was the apocalypse. I dressed for comfort, and by the way Nathan held me tightly, he didn't mind it.

I turned my head, and my nose brushed against his. My heartbeat throbbed in my throat, and every nerve I had begged me to press forward and meet his lips with mine.

Nathan was heartbreakingly beautiful. Long

eyelashes brushed his upper cheeks, and his pink lips were so full. The stubble on his cheeks and the patch of hair on his chin looked good on him. I couldn't help but reach out and run my fingers through his blonde hair.

His blue eyes popped open, and amusement spread across his face in the form of a smirk. "See something you like, killer?"

I moved my arm back, but his hand caught my wrist before he pressed a kiss to my palm. A shiver of desire raced down me at the softness of his lips.

It had been so long since I'd been in a position like this, and even with the absolute chaos outside, I wanted to close the distance between us.

"I do," I admitted in a whisper. "But I really shouldn't."

"And why not?" he murmured, breath fanning over my lips as he moved closer.

"Because I may not stay here, and if I let myself admire you the way I want to, I'll only hurt myself."

His pupils dilated before he pulled back and ran a hand down his face. He swung his legs over the side of the bed and pulled himself up with a groan. "I respect that, but we don't know what the future's going to be like. Life is short—especially now. I think it's good to act on what you want in the moment."

"I'll keep that in mind." I rubbed the sleepiness from my eyes, missing his warmth already as I climbed out of the bed and pulled the flannel down. It hit mid-thigh, so it was basically like a dress, and I felt comfortable wearing it around them.

Nathan led the way out of the room, and Calix and Micah stopped whatever discussion they were having and swept their gazes to us. Goosebumps formed on my skin the longer they stared, and it was Micah who broke the silence.

"Mornin', darlin'. Want some soup?" His gaze dropped to his flannel and up again as the warmth of the room seeped into me from the wood stove.

"Yes, please."

Calix scooped some chicken noodle soup into a bowl and passed it to me, careful not to touch my fingers as he did so.

"Thank you," I murmured, holding the warm bowl close as a shiver worked through me. "It's nice and warm."

"We all need it with the temps out now." He busied himself with making bowls for all of them, and then he placed a lid over the pot. "Winter's going to be bad."

Once everyone had their bowls, Micah, Nathan, and I went to the sofa and sat down while Calix sat on the recliner.

The warm bowl balanced on my lap as I spooned a bite and brought it to my mouth. The chicken broth coated my tongue, and the warmth spread down my throat. I sighed, feeling a small smile tug at the corners of my lips. "Thank you guys. For everything." I met Calix's gaze. "And I promise to follow all the rules you have in place to keep you comfortable."

He tilted his head, and his green eyes seemed to scrutinize me before he gave a sharp nod. "Appreciated."

Nathan set his bowl down on the end table with a sigh. "Time for coffee." He slapped his legs and got up, grabbing his empty bowl and taking it into the kitchen area to place it in a red dish bin.

"Coffee?" I perked up, continuing to eat the soup. "I haven't had coffee since six months after the apocalypse started."

"Oh, killer. I can't even imagine that," he cooed, grabbing a coffee press from the cabinet and getting to work making four cups of coffee.

"We don't have cream, but we have a little bit of sugar left," Micah told me, and my chest fluttered.

"That's amazing. Thank you!"

I finished my bowl at the same time Nathan finished making the coffees, and he gave me a mug and took my bowl with a wink.

The ceramic mug heated my palms as I cupped it and inhaled the coffee scent. "It smells so good."

"Tastes even better," Nathan mused as he sat back down. Micah grabbed his and Calix's mugs from the counter and gave Calix's his before sitting back down.

I brought the mug to my lips, and delicious hot coffee burned its way down my throat. My tongue darted across my lips. "This is so good. How do you still have coffee?"

"We go scavenging once a month to keep stock high," Micah explained, sipping on his coffee.

"Makes sense." I took another drink. "We lived off the land and only the land. Our store-bought pantry foods ended up lasting a year, but then we had to rely just on the land—which was fine since we knew how to do that anyway."

"That sounds nice," Nathan murmured.

"It was. I'm worried about the farm and our livestock," I admitted.

The guys seemed to share a look I couldn't decipher, and I bit down on my lower lip before getting to my feet, mug stashed between my hands, and walked toward the window.

The sun was high in the sky, sunbeams splashing through the room and lighting up the floors and walls. We'd slept well into the afternoon.

My body stiffened as the groans stole my attention once again. It was a tidal wave of dead, some rotten and some not, walking through to cover distance, and my skin crawled as I watched them bulldoze over most things outside to continue down their path.

They were oblivious to us up in the trees, though, and I couldn't be more grateful for that.

A blurred movement caught my eye of Spencer waving her hands in the window of the treehouse across from us, and my lips quirked into a smile… until she started making inappropriate gestures.

She moved her hands up above her head a bit and acted like she was giving hand jobs while her tongue poked into her cheek.

My face heated as I shook my head and waved my hands to make her stop.

She cackled before stopping abruptly before covering her mouth as if she'd been caught.

Dad stepped in beside her on one side with a wince as Mom stood on her other side and waved at me.

I waved back with the mug in hand, and Spencer pointed to it with a pout, making me giggle.

"What's funny, darlin'?" Micah came up beside me, waving at my family in the window.

Spencer's mouth dropped as she gestured to her shirt then Micah and me, making me glance down and realize I wore his flannel and Micah was shirtless.

I smacked a hand to my cheek and glared at her, but she just laughed. Dad was glaring at Micah, while Mom gave me a reassuring smile.

"Oh my gosh."

"They're a lively bunch," Nathan said as he stepped on my other side and waved.

Dad turned his glare to him while Mom and Spencer smiled back at him with a wave.

I spun around with one last wave and strode toward the couch. "Sorry. Spencer instigates things."

"I know. We all saw her lovely hand gestures." Nathan chuckled, and I groaned as I sipped on the coffee now that it was warm enough not to burn off my tastebuds.

"Sorry about that."

"Don't be." Micah grinned. "It's wholesome to see a full family interacting."

I smiled and stared down into the half-drank dark coffee. "Thank you."

"I'm honestly surprised you're so sweet having to live around the other two for so long," Nathan said as he sat down beside me and crossed his arms behind his head. "After the shit Daisy said to you…"

Micah's eyes darkened, while Calix's brows scrunched together.

"I can't take complete credit for being sweet." A weight pressed against my chest as my hand rose to rest on my throat. "I avoided them both like the plague. It was difficult at first, but I just spent most of my time outside with Kovu or holed up in my room."

"You were really with him for two years?" Nathan asked, and I nodded.

"How long have you known Daisy?" Micah took a swig of his coffee.

"My whole life." I stared into the darkness in my cup with a sigh. "Her mom and mine were best friends before they had us. I trusted her with everything, and when I caught them in bed together, everything I thought I knew shattered."

"They're disgusting," Calix spat the words, making my eyes snap to his as he stood up and took his coffee mug to the red bin for the dirty dishes before spinning around again. His eyes pierced mine. "I can't imagine the pain you must've gone through, but you don't have to be around them if you don't want to be."

"Kind of have to," I murmured, glancing back down at my mug. "Not like I want them dead or anything. And survival chances are better with numbers, so…"

"We can limit your interaction at least," Micah offered, and I nodded.

"They had kept their distance too throughout the years. I'm not even sure why they started to try speaking to me after so long." I winced and brought the mug to my lips before gulping the rest of the liquid.

Calix came over and reached his gloved hand out to me, and Nathan and Micah froze. "I'll take your cup."

Smiling, I placed it in his hand as my fingers met the latex and pulled back. "Thanks."

He gave me a small grunt before turning around and busying himself in the kitchen, and Micah and Nathan continued to stare at him.

"What is it?"

"He just took a mug that had your lips on it," Nathan murmured. "He won't even go near ours unless he's sprayed it first."

"He has gloves on though," I pointed out, and Micah chuckled.

"The same sentiment applies, darlin'."

The corners of my lips tugged upward. "That's sweet."

"It's somethin'," Micah mused, crossing his arms over his chest.

The rest of the day passed quickly. Micah had been checking over the interior of the treehouse, Nathan continued to go to the window and overlook the situation outside, and Calix had cleaned the entire area before going into his room and closing the door behind him.

I had asked all three of them if I could help, but they assured me they had it under control, which left me with my butt parked on the sofa, dozing off every few minutes.

It was unnerving how the commotion of the zombies outside had become a normal background noise not even after a day, but I tried not to dwell on it. Instead, I dwelled on Kovu.

My sweet, perfect horse that I had my entire life.

What happened to him had been horrific, but I knew we did the right thing, even if it made me feel like I wasn't going to recover. I pressed my palm to the center of my chest and hoped to take the pressure off of the dull throb where my heart was. Losing him *hurt*. It hurt worse than anything else I'd been through, and I hadn't even been able to properly put him to rest.

"Hey, darlin'?" Micah's raspy voice had me whipping around to see him standing next to the sofa with a medium-sized box.

"What's that?" I tossed the blanket off my lap and walked over to him. The chilly air of the treehouse gave me goosebumps after getting out from underneath the fluffy blanket.

He set it on the floor next to the sofa and opened it up to reveal a *ton* of books. "I've had this for a while now. Not sure if you're much of a reader, but it could give you something to do."

I gasped and dropped to my knees before running my fingers over the three piles of neatly stacked books within it. "May I?"

"Of course. It's why I brought it out."

I dove into it, pulling out the different books and setting them beside me as I looked through them. "I love reading," I gushed, loving the feel of the books in my hands. "But before the apocalypse, I had just finished transferring my physical library over to my kindle—big mistake, obviously. My kindle died two months into this mess. I'd just tried to save space by transferring to digital books, but I've missed falling into stories so much. I have one series still in paperback at the ranch, but I left it. I've always been a sucker for cozy romantic mystery stories, though I usually read…some other genres."

He didn't say anything, and I glanced up to find his honey brown eyes glistening with tears.

My heart thudded hard in my chest as I put the books down and climbed to my feet. "Micah…"

"I'm fine." He jerked back before running a hand down his face. "Fucking hell. I don't know why that affected me so much."

I glanced between him and the books before it clicked. "They belonged to someone special to you. Didn't they?"

He nodded, swallowing hard. "Yeah. They did."

I bit my lip and glanced down at the piles. The books were in great condition, and while the books were stories I'd be interested in, it felt wrong to read them if it caused such an emotional reaction in him.

"I appreciate you trying to help cure the boredom, but I don't think I should be reading these," I decided, crouching down and carefully putting the books back into the box.

I reached for the last book, when his calloused hand curled around my wrist.

"Stop, please," he rasped, and I froze. "I brought them out because I *want* you to read them."

"But, Micah…" I looked up into his eyes and gasped at the determination in them. "I just don't want to hurt you."

"You're not hurtin' me. You're helpin' me heal." His grip loosened as his gaze dropped down between my legs where I had them spread, showing off my panties. "Sorry." His gaze shot back up to my face, and he blushed. "Didn't mean to look."

"Don't apologize," I murmured, heat streaking through me as I closed my legs together. "I just don't want to upset you with the books."

He let me go and got up, raking his fingers through his hair with a sigh. "Sit with me?"

I grabbed the last book and put it in the box before I sat down with him on the couch.

He heaved out another breath and scratched his beard. "The books are my late fiancée's. She was an avid reader. Worked in a library even."

My chest tightened, and I reached over to grab his hand. "She had great taste in books."

He laced his fingers through mine and smiled at me. "That she did."

I squeezed his hand tight. "I'm sorry."

He shook his head and tightened his grip on my hand too. "It's been eight years now. I was twenty-six."

"If you want to talk about what happened, I'd like to hear it, but if it's too painful, I understand."

His eyes welled with tears as he stared at me. "Fuck, darlin'."

I didn't know why, but I let go of his hand and scooted closer before wrapping my arms around his waist and hugging him. "You don't have to say anything."

His arms wound around me in an instant, and my heart swelled as he buried his head in my neck and breathed.

We sat like that for a few minutes in silence, and I heard the creak of the floorboards behind us a couple of times before it went away.

"Car accident," he choked out. "I lost both my fiancée, Kelly, and my parents in one go. They were out getting snacks for a family movie night, and I was working late."

I held him close, and he did the same. "That's horrific. Did you have any other family to help you through it?"

"My sister was there. We grieved together. Kelly was her best friend. She respected my decision to move into the middle of nowhere, and I respected her decision to move to another country with her husband three years before the virus." His voice cracked. "Haven't heard from her since that first day, though."

"I wish I could take that pain away."

I knew there wasn't much I could say to help the situation. What happened was tragic, but I couldn't change it.

"Honestly, darlin'? This hug is the best source of pain relief I've felt in years."

"I'll hug you whenever you need it." I held onto him until I found myself drifting to sleep in his arms.

"Shit, Calix! Just trade me for the blue property," Nathan whined, and I stirred from my sleep.

Calix scoffed. "Not happening. I landed on it. It's mine."

"No fair!"

"Very fair, actually. It's literally part of the game."

"Micah usually trades with me."

The chest my head laid on vibrated as Micah chuckled. "Sorry. Little preoccupied to play."

"I know, and I'm jealous." Nathan huffed as I shifted up and opened my eyes with a yawn.

"How long was I out?"

"Only an hour," Micah whispered, keeping his arm around my shoulders, and I leaned back against him.

Calix and Nathan sat on the floor, a pillow under their bottoms, and played a board game.

"I love that game," I gushed. "That's awesome that you have it."

Calix's eyes lit up as he stared at me. "I love it too. My mom used to play with me every night. It was our favorite thing to do."

"That's the sweetest way to bond. My family and I had game nights growing up. After everything happened, we just kind of stopped."

Micah's hand moved from around my shoulders to my back where he began rubbing soothing motions over it. "He has to meticulously clean every piece of the game after too."

"Also something Mom and I bonded over," Calix retorted before taking his turn. "Things were definitely a lot simpler before the apocalypse though."

"Simpler?" Nathan snorted, grabbing the dice and rolling them after Calix finished moving his piece on the board. "Nah. I think it's simpler now. Back then, we had to pay bills and go to work. Now, we're just living."

"No. We're *surviving*," Calix corrected him. "We don't look forward to much except not dying now."

"I don't know. I look forward to seeing all of you now. It's not that bad." Micah shrugged.

"So many people lost their lives the first month or two when the virus spread because they lost their prescription meds," Calix stated as he collected money from Nathan.

"Sally's best friend was diabetic. She'd had a stash of insulin, but it ran out quick, and she didn't make it longer than three months with us," Nathan added with a frown.

"The government collapsed faster than most of us had expected it to," Calix added with a shiver. "I *hate* uncertainty, and the CDC was supposed to be the thing we could rely on to keep things under control with the virus, but they failed."

"That damn virus," Nathan grumbled, cursing under his breath as Calix landed on a new property to buy. "It should've never been possible. The shit we're seeing now *isn't* possible. It's like Hell on Earth."

"The virus never made any logical sense to start with." Calix's eyes darkened as he grabbed the property title. "Transmission through a bite or infected saliva into an open wound makes sense enough, but the way the zombies know how to spread it is what gets me."

"And once bitten, there's no cure." Micah shifted next to me before pulling me against his chest to wrap his arms comfortably around me. "The outbreak happened fast, but the internet hung in there for seven months, the news maybe a week, and nothing about a cure was even discussed."

"We know so little about the virus," I murmured, a chill zipping down my spine as I snuggled against Micah.

"All we know is it's twenty-four hours after the bite for death, and reanimation is twenty to thirty seconds after death," Calix said, looking pale as they took a break from the game.

"Gotta destroy the brain to kill it, just like the video games," Nathan added with a groan that mimicked the ones outside.

"And light the bodies on fire if we're around them for longer than a few hours." Calix adjusted his mask with wince. "Unlike the media representation of zombies, the real ones don't eat anything. They bite to infect and move on. I don't know which one is worse, honestly."

"These ones," Micah answered without a beat. "More infected numbers are never a good thing."

"Can't argue there."

"Scientists couldn't figure it out." I shook my head with a frown. "I'm convinced it's more supernatural than anything else at this point."

"Wouldn't surprise me," Micah grunted.

"Corpses walking around still after three years?" Nathan flattened his hands behind him on the floor and glanced back. "I'm sold with it being something science can't understand."

"I don't like it no matter what the origin is," Calix grumbled, rubbing his arms. "I'll get started on dinner. Nathan, can you clean the board and pieces?"

Nathan shot him a grin and nodded before

grabbing a purple spray bottle and cloth out of a plastic bin under the end table beside him. He sprayed the cloth and wiped everything carefully before putting it back in the box.

"What did you do before all this, killer?" Nathan asked as he got to his feet and set the board game on the end table before sinking down on the sofa beside me.

"I was a student in my last year of my agriculture degree to help with the farm." Nathan's leg rested against mine, and I found myself pushing my leg into his for the warmth. "Jay wanted me to get a business degree so I could work at his parents' firm, but I didn't like the city much. The only reason I'd been there in the first place was because of college."

"Sounds like you did what you wanted." Micah rubbed his beard. "That's good."

"I enjoyed it even with Jay's constant nagging about it." Memories of Jay trying to convince me to work at the firm flooded my brain. "He and Daisy had that in common though. She took business with him and ended up with a work study at his parents' firm. I assumed that was why they'd been getting closer that last year."

"He's an idiot." Nathan scrunched his face in disgust. "You're amazing."

"You don't even know me that well." My lips curved into an amused smile.

"I know enough." He shrugged, landing a

warm hand on my leg. "And what I know is amazing."

"Can't argue there," Micah murmured next to my ear.

They were completely unbothered by each other showing me affection, and I couldn't help but wonder why—not that I was complaining.

"Thank you both. What did you do before all this?" I waved my hand in a circle before Nathan caught it with the hand that was on my thigh and rested our joined hands back on my lap.

"I worked security for a private company," Nathan said. "I was actually working a charity event in the city when the virus hit the news. I made it back to the homestead, but I lost my entire group on the way there one way or the other. Three others survived the way out of the city with me, but we went in two different directions at the end."

"That sounds intense," I mumbled, soaking in the warmth between them. "How old are you?"

"Thirty."

"What did you do when you were living out here before this?" I asked Micah.

"Lumberjack. I worked for a company that came and got the lumber."

"Explains the muscles," I muttered to myself, and they chuckled. "What about you, Calix?"

The guys beside me stiffened, but Calix kept

stirring the pot on the wood stove like it hadn't affected him.

"Corporate work from home, and I'm twenty-seven."

"Only a year older than me," I pointed out.

"Are we too old for you?" Nathan pouted, and I giggled.

"No. None of you are," I answered honestly, and the room seemed to warm up as I wiggled between them.

"Dinner's done," Calix called out, and I scrambled up from the sofa and dashed over toward the food as I left the two chuckling men behind me.

What was wrong with me? Had it really been that long that I'm soaking up any affection thrown my way? Or was I actually connecting with them—and did they feel the same way I did?

10

NATHAN

"I'll take her to bed. I'm beat anyway." Micah scooped Tori up off the couch and cradled her sleeping form in his arms with a wink. "Good night."

She looked so serene when she was sleeping, and I couldn't get over how easy it was to be with her in our home. It was like she belonged. She was what had been missing this entire time.

"No fair." I pouted. "I wanted to take her to bed."

"You're welcome to come to bed with us when you're ready." He turned around and walked slowly into the bedroom, careful not to jostle her awake.

"Good night," I grumbled, shifting on the couch.

"Night," Calix whispered after them until they had left the room, and his eyes snapped to mine. He swallowed hard and ran a hand through his hair as he sat on the recliner. "Tori's incredibly sweet and proactive about my space. I wasn't expecting her to be so kind."

"Well of course she is." I rolled my eyes. "Micah and I wouldn't bring in someone who wouldn't respect you."

"Thanks." He went silent for a moment, his leg bouncing with nervous energy. "It's just that I've never liked anyone's presence as much as I like hers."

"Not even Micah and me?"

"Not the same way." His cheeks tinged pink as he ducked his head down. "I…almost… I think I want to *touch* her. Her hair looks so soft… At first, the germs…they made me feel *sick*, but now, as long as she's clean—and she is—I really want to hug her. Like how Micah was with her on the couch most of today, and you were cuddling her in bed this morning. It's—" He paused for a breath as he seemed to gather his thoughts. "It's hard watching you both interact with her when that's something I want to do too but can't."

My eyes widened as I stretched my arms behind my head and took in the gravity of what he was saying. Calix had *never* wanted to touch anyone before. The only person who he spoke of touching before was his mother, but even then their hugs had been very limited in his childhood since she was more of a germaphobe than he was.

"Honestly, I get it. I like her a lot too, and it's such a different feeling than anything else I've ever experienced. She's just a ray of fucking sunshine in our sad world."

"That's a great way to put it," he murmured. "Micah seems just as taken with her."

"He brought out the box of books for her." I scratched at the facial hair on my chin. "And the way they were all over each other was like they were both seeking comfort. I walked in on their conversation today accidentally, and he told her about Kelly."

His brows shot up. "Wow. He's only mentioned her in passing to us."

"I walked away before I heard too much, but he really opened up to her." I slapped my hands on my legs and got to my feet.

Since Micah went to bed with Tori, I was stuck on dish duty. I went over to the red bin and grabbed the second red bin from the shelf and brought them both into the bathroom to the sink.

I filled the dirty dish bin with soapy water and the other bin with only water before bringing them back to the kitchen and setting them on the counter. I grabbed a red kitchen towel and set it next to the bins for the dishes to dry.

Calix ambled into the kitchen area and paused a few feet from me. "How will this end?"

A lump formed in my throat as I busied my hands with scrubbing and rinsing. "With Tori?"

"Yes. I mean, us three are family now. I'd never want a woman to come between us, but Tori isn't just some woman either."

"I'm not sure if they'll go back to the ranch or not," I admitted, placing the rinsed dishes onto the towel. "I'm sure it'll be a disaster when we go check it out, but they may want to rebuild."

"But what if the horde comes through next year? Which it probably will. Wouldn't it be smarter to stay here?" He fidgeted with his gloves.

"It's something we'll have to warn them about, but it's ultimately their decision." I heaved a sigh and kept scrubbing. "As for Tori, if she does stay, I wouldn't be opposed to sharing her with you two. She obviously is interested in all of us, and we are into her too. We'd just be a bigger family."

"*Share* her?" Calix sputtered, his entire body stilling. "Oh my God, the *germs*."

I gave a weak chuckle. "It's not unheard of. We have a throuple in the Oasis, you know. Besides, you can still have your relationship with her without touching us."

He tilted his head and went quiet for a moment before nodding. "I would just have to get over your germs on her, I guess."

"If she's worth it, you'll figure it out." I finished rinsing the last dish and placed it on the towel.

"She's worth it," he murmured. "I've never had a relationship of any kind that involved touch, and she's the first person to ever make me *want* to touch her. I'll do whatever I have to—as long as she wants it too."

I smiled, grabbing the bins and walking back to the bathroom sink to dump and wash them before bringing them back to the kitchen. "Get some rest. I'm going to bed."

"Enjoy it," he called after me, and I could hear the envy in his tone.

My heart went out to him. I couldn't imagine feeling the way I do for Tori yet not being able to act on it because of an intense phobia of germs.

Calix had gotten better over the years he'd been here. At first, he refused to leave his room and had panic attacks regularly every time we'd try to check on him. He lost so much weight from not eating. But the longer he was with us, the better he adapted.

The first time he'd gone out to scavenge with us, he'd been paranoid as hell about the virus and other possible contagions. But we'd found a crossbow in packaging like new, and he learned it quickly. That way he could stay back away from the infected and shoot them that way.

He was coping, and I was grateful that he wasn't

as bad as what he said his mom was like. She wouldn't have survived this world. Not like Calix was.

My chest swelled as I stepped into the bedroom and pulled my shirt off.

Tori was fast asleep on Micah's chest, and his arm was draped around her. He stared down at her with an indiscernible look on his face, not even acknowledging me coming in.

I hadn't seen Micah like that before. We didn't know much about her, and maybe it was because we hadn't been around a single woman in a long time…but I think it was because she was something special.

I climbed into bed with them and laid down facing them. "She's perfect."

"She is," he murmured. "I want her to stay."

"We all do. Calix likes her too."

"I know. We all do, and I'm fine with that. The only thing is if she'll have us all."

My heart thudded in my chest as I stared at her. I hoped to God she ended up staying—with all of us.

11

TORI

A sickly sweet heat warmed my core as a low moan left my lips.

It had been about four years since I last had sex, but it had also been just as long since I'd been so heavily aroused.

But my dream had included the very same men I was sharing this treehouse with, and in it, we played out the dirtiest fantasies I hadn't known I was interested in.

My hand strayed between my legs before my eyes popped open, and I jerked my hand back to my chest, gasping for a breath just as I imagined Micah inside of me.

Micah and Nathan were *both* awake, staring at me with a hunger in their gazes that made my pussy throb with need.

My heart pounded relentlessly as desire skewed

my thoughts as I laid between two of the men who had been in my dream—I was only missing Calix.

"I'm so sorry," I panted the words, squeezing my eyes shut. "I… I had a dream."

"We know, darlin'," Micah rasped.

"We heard our names come out of your mouth just before you woke up," Nathan added huskily.

"That's embarrassing," I murmured, but a buzzing warmed my veins.

"No," Micah protested.

"It was hot," Nathan clarified.

Static filled my head as I reached out and touched their chests, and my actions were almost uncontrollable as a small whimper left my throat. "I haven't thought of anything remotely sexual in a long time," I admitted. "But something about you guys…"

"Same here, killer." Nathan's hand trailed up my thigh slowly, sending tingles upward. "You bring something out in us too."

"We can take care of you, if you want us to." Micah's breath hit the side of my neck, and his beard ran across the sensitive part of my collarbone. "Just a yes or no."

"Ah, yes, *please*." My tone was breathless, and my legs fell apart as Nathan's fingers hit my pussy. I gasped at the pleasure buzzing even with the barrier of my panties between us.

Micah's hot mouth parted against my neck

before his tongue swept over my sensitive skin, and my back arched.

"So responsive," Nathan teased, slipping my panties to the side before his finger pressed against my clit.

A strangled moan tore from my throat, and my legs shook from the wave of pleasure that flickered through me. "Mmf, Nathan."

"God, Tori, moan my name again." He moved his finger down to my soaked opening and dipped inside. "You're soaked."

My walls clenched his finger, pulsating around it as he pushed further. "Nathan!"

"Don't let him have all the credit, darlin'." Micah sucked on the side of my neck as his hands worked at the buttons of the flannel until he bared my breasts to both of them.

My eyes widened before he worked his way down my neck until he latched onto my nipple and sucked hard. "Micah!" I gasped as my eyes rolled back in my head, and he chuckled.

Nathan pulled his finger out only to replace it with two, and my body shuddered. "You're clamping so tight on my fingers. Can't imagine how good you'd feel on my cock."

Micah's hand grasped my other breast, rolling my nipple between his fingers and making the pressure inside of me so heavy. "You are beautiful."

The new sensation of both of them on me, *pleasuring me*, sent me reeling.

Nathan curled his fingers just as Micah bit down on my nipple, and my nerve endings exploded.

I cried out as stars filled the back of my eyelids, and my body shook with the wave of the first orgasm I'd had in *years*. I rode out the liquid ecstasy flooding my system, and I sucked in a large breath before my eyes flew open and connected with wide green eyes.

Calix stood in the doorway, frozen to the spot as he stared at the three of us.

"Calix?" I murmured, chest heaving up and down as my thoughts started to clear.

He blinked a few times before he stumbled back and scrambled out of the room with a sharp breath.

I shot up and closed the flannel around me before running a hand through my hair. "I am *so* sorry."

"Sorry?" Nathan shook his head before removing his fingers and bringing them to his mouth and sucking them. "I'm not. You took what you wanted, and we were happy to give it."

Heat streaked through me as I ducked my head, but Micah gripped my chin between his index finger and thumb and turned me to look at him. His eyes burned with heat. "Don't apologize. I loved every minute of that."

"But Calix…" My lips curled downward.

Micah reluctantly let go of me with a sigh. "I'll go talk to him." He hauled himself out of bed and grabbed his sweats before shoving his legs through and pulling them up. "He's probably just embarrassed."

I fumbled with the bottom of the flannel before trying to button them up, my face flaring with heat as I tried to control my breathing. "I—"

"That better not be another apology." Nathan sighed and knocked my hands out of the way before buttoning it up the rest of the way, then he cupped my face in his hands and forced me to look at him. "Calix is going to be fine, and so are we. More than fine, really."

"Don't stress about it, darlin'," Micah murmured before heading out of the room.

"How can I not?" I mumbled, and Nathan leaned forward to meet my lips with his.

His lips were soft, and his tongue glided over the seam of my lips before I parted them. Our tongues twirled around each other, as I wrapped my hands around his wrists and moaned into his mouth. He kissed me tenderly, almost as if he was trying to show me that whatever this was between us was *more* than physical attraction.

Pulling back, he kissed my nose before resting his forehead against mine. "I *like* you, killer. Micah is so into you that he can't take his eyes off of you, and Calix likes you so much he's been thinking of *hugging* you. That's big for all of us. I know you don't know us all that well, and maybe we *are* jumping the gun a little bit, but…"

I swallowed the heavy lump in my throat, and his palms were so warm against my cheeks. "But what?"

"Let's head out there." He pulled back, and the cold air of the room replaced where his hands had been, and he got out of bed before tugging a long-sleeved shirt over his head from his dresser and tossing me a pair of sweatpants.

I took them and got out of bed before putting them on and tying them tightly. "Thank you."

He held his hand out to me before lacing his fingers in mine and tugging me into the living room where Calix and Micah were waiting.

The atmosphere was tense as we went in and sat on the sofa next to Micah, me in the middle. Calix sat straight on his recliner, and I could practically feel the nervous energy wafting off of him.

"I'll be blunt," Micah said, scratching his beard as his gaze locked on mine. "All three of us are interested in you."

"Interested how?" My throat tightened, and I was *well aware* of their eyes on me.

Even with the undead horde making noise under us, I wasn't the least bit scared or nervous about the state of the situation or the world. The only focus I had in that moment was on the three men in this room with me.

"Romantically," Calix answered.

"And sexually, obviously." Nathan winked, and I groaned before covering my face with my hands. "I'll let you take a minute to think that over while I get us coffee."

The couch shifted as he got up, and static filled my ears as I thought about what that meant.

They were *all three* interested romantically and sexually, in me.

I already knew I was attracted to all of them, but what exactly were they asking? Did they want us to start dating? If so, what were the rules of having such a dynamic in a relationship?

My head reeled with so many what-ifs, but more than the indecision, I *wanted* to try it.

The smell of coffee filled my nose, and I slid my hands down my face to see the coffee mug being held in front of my face.

"Thanks." I smiled and took the cup from Nathan, and he finished passing the mugs around before taking his seat next to me.

"What're you thinking?" Calix's leg bounced uncontrollably, and his fist was tightened on his knee.

"Um… I've only really known you guys a couple of days, and before I met you three, I hadn't thought of being with someone else after the mess that happened with Jay. I had practically given up on the idea of finding anyone else, especially the way the world is. But even when I was with Jay, I didn't feel the same desire I feel about you three. Sure, sexually, but more than that. I actually really enjoy being around you. Maybe it's because it's new and exciting, but I think it's something more. What I really need to know is what you three expect of this now."

Calix's eyes lit up, and even though his mouth was covered with a mask, I could tell he was smiling. "I want to be with you. Like in a relationship."

"All three of you do?" I moved my gaze toward Micah, who nodded.

"Yes. I want to date you."

Nathan chuckled as I turned to him. "Of course we want to date you, killer. All three of us."

"Exclusively?" I nibbled on my lip, and their faces darkened.

"Yes," Calix said. "Just the four of us."

"And you three are okay with, um, me and you three?"

"Yes, darlin'. We are more than okay with sharing you between the three of us exclusively." Micah's large hand landed on my thigh.

"We do want to make it clear now though." Nathan's hand curled around my other thigh. "It's just us. No one else. No other men or women would ever be added to this relationship. It's unconventional, but we would still be committed to just you, and you would be committed only to the three of us."

"And all three of you are truly okay with that?" I glanced at Calix, clutching the mug tightly with sweaty palms.

He had been the one I hadn't had much time with. The one who I knew had an issue with touch. The fact he'd been included in this had been both surprising and exciting, and I was excited to learn even more about it.

"Yes," he confirmed. "Are you okay with being committed to us only?"

"Of course." My heart pounded loudly, and I took a sip of the coffee. "Dating in the apocalypse is unconventional anyway, right?"

"Absolutely." Nathan chuckled.

I settled back against the sofa with the coffee held up to my nose as I basked in the warmth of the cup. "How long do you think we'll be stuck up here?"

"I don't know," Micah groaned, getting to his feet and walking across the wooden floor that creaked with every other step as he went toward the window. It had become a charm of the treehouse that I found comfort in.

I got up and followed him, finding amusement in the creaks of the boards as I made my way toward him to look out the window.

The fear that hung over my head was muted as I stared down at the shambling rotten horde below the trees. I knew it should've been terrifying. We were essentially stuck up here, but being with these three men in this room... I didn't feel the fear I knew I should.

Instead, my mind buzzed, blocking out everything except the low, pleasant hum of excitement for the future and the relationship I was developing with them.

"Seems like they're thinning out a bit." Micah crossed his arms as he stared down at them surging forward on a mission, all of them.

A shiver tore through me, and I wrapped my arms around my middle. "Does that mean it's almost over?"

Strong arms wrapped around me from behind as Nathan pressed a kiss to my neck and held me close. "Almost, killer."

I glanced up at the window and froze as I noticed Jay standing in the window of their treehouse, gaze locked on me.

"I'd say a couple more days at least." Micah leaned forward, taking my attention from Jay, and kissed my forehead. "Don't worry, darlin'. Riding this out won't be so bad now that you're here."

"I'm glad I met you." My skin tingled with their touch, and I didn't bother glancing at Jay as we left the window and went back to sit on the sofa.

"What about me?" Nathan teased, grabbing my hand and flipping it over to rest on his leg as he traced invisible lines up and down my forearm. "Are you glad you met me?"

"I'm happy that I met all of you, obviously." My cheeks burned as I grinned and leaned against Micah. "What happens after the horde passes?"

"We have to check our land and belongings. The shed, supplies, and the other survivors," Micah explained. "We keep supplies in the two utility sheds under the large trees just a few meters away from the shower shed. The horses were put in the large reinforced one, so we will check on them as well."

I tensed, but Nathan's continuous glide of his fingers on my skin relaxed me again. "Do you think the horses will be okay? They haven't been confined for so long before. I'm sure they're scared."

"I think we've done everything we can to protect that shed. We can't see it from the treehouse, but I'm assuming they're okay. I haven't heard the zombies attack anything so far," Nathan told me as I brought the mug up to my lips and drank the last bit of it.

Calix got up and took my cup as Nathan placed his on the end table next to Micah's. "Benjamin checks the water supply and river."

"Where's the water supply?"

He placed my cup in the red bin and came back to his recliner. "He has several. Two in the big shed, one in the small shed, and a tank below each treehouse. He takes it very seriously, and it makes me feel comfortable about our drinking and bathing water. Which says a lot about his proactiveness."

"After the Oasis is safe, are you accompanying us to the ranch? Or are we going to be on our own heading back?"

My question made the men tense, and I shifted in the seat with the uncomfortable silence.

"You're going back then?" Micah asked, and I frowned as Nathan stopped rubbing my arm.

"Um… I don't know. My parents and Spencer are my family, and living so far away from them when the world is like this makes me nervous," I admitted. "But at the same time, I don't want to leave you three behind. I mean, we are dating, right?"

"We are," Nathan murmured. "And I'm sure I speak for all of us when we say we don't want you to leave."

"But we also understand moving in with us after a couple of days is a little too much to ask," Micah added, his brows scrunched together as if the thought pained him. "We'll figure out a way to make it work, but I'm going to be honest with you, there's a good chance the ranch will not have made it."

I pulled my hands into my lap and sighed. "I know…"

"But whatever happens, you still have us," Calix said, his face turning pink as he clasped and unclasped his hands together.

"Thank you." I swallowed the thickness in my throat and smiled at them. "I appreciate you three being so sweet."

"We appreciate you giving us a chance. I know I do," Calix murmured. "But you should know that I haven't ever touched someone in a romantic sense, and while I do want to touch you… I don't know if I'm capable of giving you what Micah and Nathan can—physically. I couldn't even watch porn before all of this happened because it made me nauseous."

"That's okay," I assured him, wanting nothing more than to hug him to let him know how I feel but knowing that would be too much. "We can go as slow as you need to, and if you can only be with me without physical touch, that's fine too. I don't mind. I mean… I *do* want to be able to touch you, but I also understand that it makes you uncomfortable. I'll never make you go outside your comfort zone, Calix."

"Thank you, Tori," he whispered lowly.

We went into a comfortable silence after that, and we ate some canned vegetables for dinner. Micah had insisted I read a book after we ate, so I chose one out of the box and read most of the evening before getting tired.

The three of us even waved to my parents who we'd caught in the window before going to bed.

I fell asleep snuggled between Micah and Nathan, and slept amazing until a sharp pain lanced at my bladder.

As I slipped out of bed, Nathan woke up, rubbing his eyes. "Where are you going?"

"I have to pee. Go back to bed." I went to his side and kissed his lips softly.

He gave me a grunt of acknowledgment before passing back out, and I tip-toed through the living room.

Calix had insisted that we needed to keep the door shut constantly to avoid spreading germs into the other living areas, so I didn't think anything of it when I opened the door to see Calix standing in the bathroom with a candle set on top of the sink. A soft flicker of the wick lit up the room, exposing Calix's naked, soaped up body—without his mask on.

And by gods, he was *stunning*.

His nose was straight, and his jawline was sharp. His muscles were carved out clearly with a V leading down to his large, erect cock. He looked even better naked in real life than he did in my dream.

My mouth fell open, and my pussy clenched at the sight.

A squeal tore from his throat before he stepped

forward and slipped, his body smacking into mine, slamming us both into the living room floor with him on top of me.

Desire thrummed through me like electricity, and I bit my lip to stifle the moan as his cock rested between my legs, rubbing against my thin cotton panties.

He pushed himself up with his hands, leaning over me close enough for his breath to fan over my face, and heat pooled between my legs.

My heart pounded relentlessly against my breast bone as he stared down at me with his perfect face and soft-looking lips. "Calix…"

"Tori," he murmured, his voice sounding way huskier than I'd ever heard before.

Feet pounded against the ground as Micah's gruff voice called out, "What's going on?"

Calix and I both snapped our attention to the two men barely dressed with weapons, storming in.

Nathan's laughter pierced the room, and Calix quickly pushed up off of me and covered himself with his hands.

"How did that happen?" Nathan howled.

"It's my fault," Calix and I said at the same time, and we swung our gazes to each other. "No, it's mine. I'm sorry!"

Micah joined in with Nathan's giggle episode, and we groaned.

"I'm sorry for walking in on you." I ran a hand

down my face before getting to my feet. "And for you touching me."

"No. I'm sorry. I woke up from a night terror drenched in sweat and wanted to wash. I shouldn't have been so startled I slipped. I apologize for knocking you down. I...actually didn't mind touching you."

"We can see that," Nathan teased him, placing his gun down on the end table with a yawn. "I'm going back to sleep, but just for the record, it's not fair that you're that big."

Calix's eyes widened, but he didn't reply.

"Just happy everyone's fine. Night," Micah grumbled, running a hand down his face and set his axe on the ground leaning against the end table. He pressed a kiss to my head before heading back to the bedroom.

I arched a brow at Nathan, who shrugged. "Micah's grumpy when he doesn't get enough sleep. Night, killer. We'll be waiting for you."

"Night," I whispered as Nathan followed Micah back to bed, and I faced Calix again. I trembled with nervousness and maybe a little excitement from being so close to him. "Do you need help?"

"Um, not help, but you could stay and talk to me." He stopped covering himself and scratched the back of his neck.

"Of course." I leaned against the door frame and tried to be respectful by not looking down at his erection as he got back to washing himself. "I'm sorry though, truly."

"Don't be." He blushed.

"Did you want to talk about the night terror? When I have them, it helps to talk about them."

He shook his head, and his expression darkened. "I was at the hospital when the virus spread. I hunkered down there for a year and a half before Micah and Nathan found me. I saw some *terrible* things that I'd rather forget."

"Why were you at the hospital?"

He began to lather his leg as he scrunched his face up in a wince. "I bought hospital grade protective gear and cleaning supplies. It was cheaper to buy from the hospital than the company, so I did it every month."

"That makes sense. I'm sorry you had to be there of all places."

He switched legs and glanced up to meet my gaze. "Me too. It was a miracle I survived. Believe it or not, but I hid out in the *morgue* with another guy. We did what we could with what we had. The zombies didn't stick around after they'd infected what they had thought was everyone in the building, so scavenging was the most difficult thing."

"What happened with the other guy?"

He glanced down and placed the sudsy wash cloth in the sink before grabbing a clean one and dunking it in the clean water. He ran the wet cloth over his soapy areas to rinse, and we fell into a tense quiet as he rinsed off. When he finished, he dumped the bins in the sink and placed them in the cabinet before spraying them and placing the wash cloths in another bin.

I grabbed a towel off the hook next to the door and handed it to him.

He hesitated for only a split second before taking it and drying off.

Wrapping the towel around his waist, he came closer. "That guy shot himself in the head with a gun we'd taken from the security office. He did it when I was asleep, and I woke up next to him covered in his blood."

The anguish on his face made my heart twist in my chest. "Holy shit, Calix. That's a nightmare."

"Literally." He paused and stepped closer. "I have that same night terror every other night. It was hard losing the only other survivor I had around, but his blood caked on me is something I can *still feel.*"

"I wish I could do something."

"You already have. I've not even told Micah or Nathan yet, and somehow telling you, I feel better." He swallowed, his Adam's apple bobbing.

"I'll always listen to you," I promised, and it *killed* me not to wrap my arms around him.

His gaze dropped down to my lips, and he bit down on his lip. "Can I try something?"

"Anything."

"Will you brush your teeth and wipe your mouth off?"

I arched my brows but nodded and moved around him to the sink. Grabbing my toothbrush out of its plastic baggie, I used the toothpaste and brushed my teeth more thoroughly than I think I'd ever done before.

"Here." He handed me a cloth, and I used it to wash my face and lips before rinsing and drying.

I turned to face him, and his face had paled. "Calix?"

"I desperately want to kiss you, but I don't know if…"

"You don't have to," I told him firmly, tightening my fist to stop myself from reaching out and touching him. "I'll still like you no matter what."

"And that just makes me want to even more." His eyes had darkened as he stared at my lips. "Let me touch you. Let me kiss you, but please, don't touch me back."

I threaded my fingers together and kept my hands in front of me. "I won't touch you."

He sucked in a hitched breath before leaning in so slowly, I thought I'd pass out from the anticipation. His warm, soft lips covered mine, and my body flooded with belonging.

Every part of me wanted to tug him closer, but I kept my hands pressed against my body to avoid it.

He slowly moved his lips against mine, and I followed his lead. His fingertips trailed down my cheek as he pressed three long, tender kisses to my lips and pulled back. "That was my first kiss, and I never thought I'd be able to do that."

"But you did, and it was perfect," I whispered, and he pulled back.

My heart ached at the way he moved back, but I understood why he did it. Kissing was a *huge* step, and I would take that win and bask in it for days from now.

"Let me walk you to bed," he murmured, and my body jolted as my bladder prodded at me.

"I have to use the toilet first. I forgot I had woken up to pee." My face streaked with heat, and he shook his head.

"I'm sorry. I didn't mean to make you wait." He stepped out. "I'll be here when you're done."

I nodded and shut the door behind me. I let out a long breath as reality hit me. I'd kissed Calix, and his lips were *so soft*.

Pushing down my excitement, I used the bathroom and made sure to properly clean it before washing my hands and opening the door.

Calix stood with sweats, a shirt, and a mask back on.

A small pang of disappointment stabbed at me, and I tried to brush it away as he led me back to the bedroom and paused at the doorway.

"I will work on having you come into my space, but I'm not there yet." He tugged at his collar, and I shook my head with a small smile.

"Take your time, Calix. I'm not going anywhere."

"Good night, honey. Sleep well," he murmured, leaning closer as if he wanted to kiss me again and then turning on his heels back to his room.

My chest swelled with a buzzing warmth as I slid in between Micah and Nathan.

Sure, the world had ended and zombies had taken over—but I was safe, and I had three boyfriends who made me happier than I had been before the apocalypse.

12

TORI

"It's always the one you don't expect," I grumbled, flipping the page of the book and reading the scene with palpable tension.

The wife wasn't murdered by her husband like I'd expected, *no*. It was her neighbor. The nice lady who she had become fast friends with after she moved next door *only two months prior*. She'd been fast to comfort the husband, and I had truly thought she was just being neighborly, but that wasn't her intention.

No. She wanted the husband all to herself, and she didn't care what she had to do as long as she got what she wanted in the end.

A bitter taste rose on my tongue as I read on, only feeling slightly better when she confessed everything and tried to kill the husband when the cops had been in the next room without her knowing.

I slammed the book shut with a huff and sat it back in the box.

"Not a good ending?" Micah's brow rose from next to me.

He, Nathan, and Calix sat in the living room with me, and aside from their side conversations, they'd pretty much been staring at me. I had read through the entire novel since that morning, and the sun had already started to set.

"Something like that," I murmured as I wrinkled my nose.

A dull orange slipped through the window, and Micah got up and lit the two candles in the room to give some more light.

"The zombies have almost passed through." Nathan stretched his arms over his head before settling back against the sofa.

"When do you think we'll be able to go down?" I asked, watching the flick of the flame on the candle next to me.

"Probably tomorrow." Calix got up and went to his room only to return a few seconds later with the board game they'd been playing. He placed a pillow down for himself and sat down.

"Ready to get your ass beat again?" Nathan snickered as he slid off the couch and pulled me down with him.

Micah came down too, and we all moved to one side of the board.

"It's really cool how well you guys play this game. Like you already know which player you are and which side you want." I grinned as I took the last little tin game piece in the shape of a horse.

"And now we have you with us," Calix murmured, his eyes glistening as he stared at me. "My mom used to play as the horse. It's really good to see you using it."

My lips quirked into a smile as I placed the horse at the start block with the rest of them. "She sounds fun."

"She was, but she didn't let herself have fun any other time. Only when we played this game." He went quiet and handed everyone a small pack of two dice. "She's why there are so many precautions in place for it. These baggies make sure everyone has their own dice. Mine are the green, Micah's are the red, Nathan's the blue, and yours is the yellow now."

I nodded, slipping the dice out of the baggie and into my palm. "Thank you. That's really nifty."

"My mom was diagnosed with mysophobia—being afraid of germs—a few months after she had me. She'd been diagnosed with OCD a few years before she met my father." He scrunched his nose in disgust at mentioning his father and rolled his dice.

The dice hit the board with two thumps, and he

moved his piece onto a property that he bought, paying the *banker*, which was Nathan.

"What caused the onset of mysophobia?" I asked as Micah took his turn, paying for a property and taking the deed.

"She had an emergency c-section with me, and it was considered a traumatic birth for reasons she never disclosed to me." His eyes were trained on the board as he talked, and his voice wobbled. "Her sutures got severely infected, and she was admitted into the hospital for a week. After that, she couldn't stand any germs. My father lasted two months after she came home before up and leaving us both without so much as a goodbye."

"I'm so sorry that happened, Calix. He sounds like an awful person. I know that was probably hard to talk about, so thank you for telling me."

He shrugged, and Nathan took his turn only to land on the property Micah had just bought.

"No! Come on! It's my first turn." Nathan pouted, shooting Micah puppy dog eyes.

"Pay up," Micah grumbled, holding his hand out for the money, which made Nathan whimper like a hurt animal as he stared at his money.

Something I liked about Calix's version of the game was that there weren't bills but rather plastic colored coins. Red was a million, blue was one-hundred-thousand, green was ten-thousand, yellow was thousand, silver was one-hundred, purple was ten, and orange was one. Easier to clean and keep better track of.

Nathan dropped his pleading face and grabbed a coin before dropping it into Micah's hand. "No fun."

"Very fun," Micah clarified, and I swore I saw a twinkle in his eye.

"Your turn, honey," Calix murmured, and I smiled before rolling the dice.

"Honey? That's cute." Nathan grinned.

"It's comforting." I moved my piece to what happened to be an expensive property and paid for it before getting the deed.

"How so?" Micah asked as Calix took his turn.

"My dad calls me honeybee. Just makes me feel at home," I tried explaining the warm, fuzzy static that filled me when Calix called me honey.

"That's cute." Micah rolled his dice and claimed another property. "I'm so glad you came with us, darlin'."

"Thank you for giving us that option."

"We don't usually do what we did for you." Nathan landed only a space from the one I claimed and had to pay the bank for a card he'd pulled on that spot. "This is going to be a rough game for me."

"Bad luck?" I rolled my dice and claimed a few more moves that landed me on a property that I bought. "Regardless, I'm happy you decided to intervene on our behalf before you knew us. I can imagine everyone has lost their morals the way the world is."

"You have no idea, and I'm glad we intervened too," Nathan muttered bitterly.

Calix landed on Micah's property and handed him a coin while Micah smirked and proceeded to roll his dice and buy a new property.

"What do you mean?" I asked, and he rolled again, landing on a property next to mine that was still open.

His lips curved into a small smile as he bought the property, but his eyes darkened. "What happened to my family's homestead was my fault, but because of what I did, we learned why we had to be so cautious with others."

"If it was someone else who did it, I don't see how that's your fault." My dice hit the board with two small thumps, and I moved to another new property in the same area as Calix's and bought it.

Nathan sighed, running a hand through his hair before shifting his legs to the side. "We stayed at the homestead one entire year before I fucked up, and it was almost like we had been in a bubble, similar to your ranch, really."

Calix took his turn and landed on a card block, and the card gave him five more red coins.

"Bubbles are great until they're popped," I murmured, and Nathan gave me a weak smile with a nod as Micah took his turn, landing on Nathan's property and paying him what he was owed.

"Exactly. Only my actions are what popped ours." Nathan took the coin from Micah and rolled his dice, earning another property. "We were out looking for other survivors. We wanted to help people."

"And you found someone?" I took my turn, and landed on Calix's property, paying him and keeping my eyes glued to Nathan as I waited for him to continue.

"Yeah. I did. It was a woman only a year or so younger than me. She'd been fending off a zombie with her high heel, and I was an idiot. I saved her, and we took her back with us. She managed to charm me enough to tell my dad he was paranoid instead of believing him when he told me something wasn't right with her." His lips curved down in a harsh frown. "But I had wanted her to stay with us, and I was blinded by the possibility of romance. That night, we slept together, and when I woke up, raiders were attacking in the middle of the night. She had been with them and led them straight to our home. They tried to kill us, but my dad had an escape route mapped out."

"That sounds more like her fault than yours, Nathan." I reached over and grabbed his hand to squeeze, and he squeezed back. "You had gone out looking for survivors, and you did what you had thought was right. She manipulated you. You can't fault yourself for being compassionate and hopeful."

"But Dad knew something was wrong. If I hadn't been so blinded—"

"But you were, and what happened *happened*. You can't do that to yourself, Nathan. Besides, look at what happened after. You have Micah and Calix, *and me*. Plus, we live in the best possible place to live in the apocalypse. These treehouses are sturdy and far up away from zombies."

"See, we told you that," Calix added.

"Told ya so," Micah agreed.

Nathan's frown faded as a smile replaced it, and he grabbed my hand tighter before jerking me up and into his lap, careful of the board in front of us as I squealed.

His warm lips met mine, and my legs dropped to either side of his lap. He trailed his hands down my sides until he grabbed my ass, and I pushed myself down enough to feel his hardness between his legs, making him moan.

"Wow," Calix choked out, and Micah chuckled.

A loud, guttural roar shook the treehouse, and Nathan and I broke apart just as the roar turned to a high-pitched shriek.

"What the fuck was that?" Nathan pulled me to my feet as Micah and Calix jumped up.

"Sounded like a mountain lion." Micah's jaw tightened.

My ears hurt from the sound as adrenaline pumped into me, and we all rushed to the window to stare into the darkness as the shriek settled, replaced by whimpers before it went away completely.

Goosebumps covered my arms, and dread coiled in my gut as my hand clamped over my mouth.

Calix wrapped his arms carefully around my shoulders and leaned me into his chest as terror rooted me to the spot. "It's okay, honey. We're safe up here. Micah made this treehouse tough. Everything's locked up."

"What kind of wildlife is around here?"

"Bears, coyotes, rattle snakes, wolves now, and mountain lions are the most dangerous animals around here. But I've noticed a lot of out of place predatory animals since the apocalypse. Though, we haven't seen snakes in a while now. Still watch out for them though, obviously."

I nodded. "That's terrifying."

"That mountain lion we heard must've been bitten," Nathan stated the obvious, and Calix stiffened further as he pulled away.

Micah dragged me into his arms, and his woodsy scent filled my senses as I snuggled closer to him, already missing Calix even as I savored

Micah's warmth. "We'll keep an eye out and tell the others, though, I'm sure they came to that conclusion on their own."

Watching out for zombies and wildlife was something I had become accustomed to at the ranch the past three years, but watching out for zombified wildlife was something else entirely.

We left the window and cleaned up the game and house before heading to bed, and as soon as I was tucked between Micah and Nathan, sleep took over, and my worries were mercifully put on pause.

13

MICAH

Waking up next to Tori had become something I looked forward to in the past few days.

Ever since I lost Kelly and my parents, waking up was my least favorite part of the day. It was lonely, more so than at night when I could fall asleep and ignore the world. Now that Tori had come into the picture, I had both her and Nathan to wake up to rather than myself. It was something I hadn't realized I needed, and now that she was here, I didn't want to let her go.

My cock dug into her stomach as she draped herself over me, and Nathan's arm was wound around her waist. She was so beautiful it made my chest ache, and it made me *want* in a way I never had before.

I couldn't stop my hips from bucking slightly, and Tori moaned, picking up her head and catching my lip with hers in a searing kiss as if she'd been awake for a minute. A jolt of desire worked its way through me as I moved Nathan's arm from her, and I gripped her ass before flipping her over and pinning her to the bed.

The bed creaked from the movement, and she relaxed as I grabbed her wrists and held them above her head. I broke the kiss and stared down at her. My heart was like a fist pounding in my chest from the way her body reacted to me.

Tori was intoxicating. She was healing all the pieces of me I thought were lost, and I desired her so desperately it *hurt*. Her blue eyes were dark with need as she stared back up at me, her chest heaving with every breath.

My fingers worked at the flannel's buttons, and they trailed between the fabric up toward her breasts and pushed it away. "So beautiful, darlin'," I rasped, leaning down and nuzzling her breasts, licking and sucking at her nipples.

She arched, a breathy moan pulling from her throat. "Micah, *oh my God*!"

I swore I hardened even further with my name leaving her mouth, and my thumb and index finger teased the hardened nipple of her other breast. Letting go of her wrists, I gave one last suck to her nipple before helping her sit up and take off her clothes.

"Well, fuck. Good morning, killer—and Micah. Best wakeup call ever," Nathan croaked, rubbing his eyes and undressing himself as Tori pulled my boxers down, springing my throbbing cock free.

"Morning, handsome." Tori's eyes slid toward Nathan, and with a sultry smile, she leaned forward, her hand curling around the base of my cock, and wrapped her lips around the tip.

I groaned, pleasure spreading through me as she took me into her mouth. She slowly bobbed her head, eyes locked with Nathan as she worked me.

"Holy fuck, Micah. She's fucking perfect." Nathan's mouth hung open as he watched her hungrily suck my cock. "You're sucking him so good, killer. He looks like he's going to bust."

Her eyes shifted to me, and my cock twitched as she flattened her tongue on the underneath of me and moaned. The vibration of it coaxed me to my climax, and I pulled out of her mouth, bunching her hair in my fists and dragging her up.

"Not yet, darlin'. I want to be inside you." I crashed my lips on hers, and her arms flew around my neck as she kissed me with passion. Her tongue swirled around mine, and I palmed her ass, loving the way it felt in my hands.

"I'd apologize for breaking that up, but I'm not

sorry. I need to taste you." Nathan slipped his arms around her waist and tugged her until she fell back on the bed again, legs spread and pussy glistening with her desire for me—for us.

"I'm not mad at getting a show." My lips quirked into a smirk, and Tori's legs trembled as my gaze bore into her.

She was a goddess. I'd never been so turned on in my entire life.

Nathan wasted no time, gripping her thighs and diving between them. He latched onto her clit, and her body jerked, eliciting a pleasure-filled yelp.

His fingers slipped inside of her, and she threw her head back. "You're too good at that!"

He chuckled but didn't stop pleasuring her with his mouth and fingers.

My cock throbbed painfully as she threaded her fingers in his hair with one hand and grabbed her breast with the other.

I moved toward her and knocked her hand off her breasts, replacing it with my mouth and kneading the other breast with my hand. She shook violently under the flood of pleasure, moaning out in bliss.

When the trembling stopped, I kissed her breasts and moved as Nathan popped his head up and met her gaze before sucking the fingers he had inside of her.

"You're sweet," he murmured.

"Come here. Let me taste you. It's only fair," she told him.

"And what about me, darlin'?"

"You said you wanted to be inside of me. I can do both, can't I?" She slowly turned herself onto all fours, and I threw my head back with a groan at how perfect she looked on all fours with her soaked pussy spread for me.

"Fuck," Nathan moaned, rushing to his knees in front of her, and she wrapped her hand around his cock, pumping him slowly.

"I'll pull out," I promised, grabbing a handful of her ass and kneading it. "Are you sure this is what you want?"

"More than anything," she panted, and I grabbed my cock, nudging the tip against her drenched opening.

I slid in with little resistance because of how wet she was, but her walls squeezed me tightly with every inch I pushed in until I bottomed out, and she spasmed around me with a moan.

"You feel so good," she gasped, and Nathan moaned as she licked up his length.

"You feel like paradise," I groaned.

She took him in her mouth with a series of moans and whimpers as I pulled back slowly, feeling her ripple and stretch around me before plunging in deep.

"She's everything," Nathan gasped, threading his fingers in her hair.

I started to thrust harder, pounding into her heat as she took us both eagerly. She used one hand to prop herself on the bed and the other on his thigh. "She's taking me so good. I'm going to need to pull out."

She moaned, making a sound of protest around his cock, and I slowed my strokes as Nathan tensed, filling the room with a loud moan as he came in her mouth.

He slipped out of her mouth, and she gasped. "Don't stop, Micah." Her head fell onto the mattress as she picked her ass up and slammed herself back against me. "Come inside of me if you want. Just please fuck me harder!"

"And now I'm getting hard again," Nathan stated, dropping onto his back as he watched us. "You did such a good job, killer."

"Are you sure?" I kept my strokes slow in case she changed her mind, feeling her pussy spasm around me in desperation.

"More than sure, Micah, *please,*" she whimpered. "I'm infertile so we don't have to worry about pregnancy."

That was enough for me.

"Hang on tight, darlin'." I tightened my hold on her hips and drove into her with abandon, loving the way she gripped my cock as I did it.

Her hands clutched the bed sheets as screams tore out of her, and she kept her ass up as her pussy clenched tighter around me until I could barely thrust. Her screams turned raspy to moans as she came, and as she rode down the climax, I picked my pace back up until my orgasm exploded.

I spilled inside of her, and my vision blackened at the edges as I came with a loud groan.

I'd never come inside of anyone before, but I couldn't deny how *intimate* it was. Carefully, I pulled out of her, and my cock was drenched from both of our cum.

Tori dropped flat on the bed with a pleased sigh as Nathan handed me a cum rag, his name for it, to wipe myself and Tori of the mess. Calix had designated each of us two of them for masturbation clean up, which I understood him not wanting cross-contamination.

Nathan helped Tori turn over, and I spread her legs to clean my cum from between her folds as it dripped out of her.

"Calix," she murmured, staring at the door.

I glanced over to see him standing at the doorway, his eyes heated as he stared at her.

"Enjoy the show?" Nathan teased.

Calix cleared his throat before turning on his heels and walking out of the room in haste.

"Stop teasing him," Tori murmured, her body

flush from the activity. "Thank you both for being so sweet."

"Thank you for the awesome blowjob, killer." Nathan gave her a lopsided grin as I finished cleaning her up and helping her into her panties.

"Thanks for the great head, handsome." She winked, and I chuckled, making her attention fall to me. "And thank you for the mind-blowing sex, darling."

"Darling, hmm?" I grabbed a clean flannel and helped her into it, and Nathan buttoned it for her. "I like it."

"You call me darlin'. I figured darling was appropriate." She smiled at me, and my chest tightened.

"You're so pretty," I blurted, and pink cascaded over her cheeks.

"And you're handsome."

"I thought I was handsome?" Nathan pouted, and she giggled.

"You both are."

"This is by far the most fun I've had since the apocalypse." Nathan got out of bed and got dressed before helping her out of bed and kissing her lips softly. "You're the best thing that has happened to me since this happened."

"I feel the same way about you three," she murmured, kissing him again.

I got up and got dressed before we made our way out of the bedroom. Calix sat on his recliner with his head in his hands. Four full bowls of beef stew were on the counter, and the wood stove had been turned off already.

"Good morning, Calix," Tori said softly as she sat on the sofa, fussing with the end of the flannel. "I'm sorry you walked in on that."

"Don't be," he croaked. "You're stunning. And things I had thought were disgusting before have become more intriguing. I thought sex would be something I would never be interested in, but after seeing *that* this morning... I want to be able to do that. Not all together. I don't think I'll be ready for that for a long time. But with *you*. So long as we've washed first."

"I understand, and I would like that. But we can go at your pace," she told him, and his shoulders deflated as the tension around him seemed to melt away.

I grabbed her bowl and mine as Nathan washed his hands before he grabbed his and Calix's and went to the living room. We handed them their bowls, and we fell into a comfortable silence as we ate.

After we had finished, I gathered the dishes and washed them since we had forgotten to do them last night.

Nathan called Tori to the window, and she and Calix went over.

"The horde must've fully passed last night," he said, pointing out. "We'll need to go out and kill off any stragglers."

"How many are there usually?" she asked.

"No more than twenty. Usually."

"*Twenty?* That's a horde in itself."

"Not anymore," Calix grumbled. "The longer we live in a zombie-infested world, the more zombies come to be."

"I guess," she sighed.

I finished up the last of the dishes, and the three of them were pacing the living room.

There was a restless feeling in the air, and after being in the treehouse waiting out the horde, we were all ready to get outside and breathe the fresh air.

I grabbed my axe off the floor in the living room, and Tori grabbed her golf club from beside the door. Nathan went into my bedroom closet to grab his sniper rifle, and Calix went to his room to grab his crossbow.

"Ready, darlin'?" I pressed a kiss to her temple, and she nodded, but a frown marred her blissful happiness from earlier that morning.

"What's wrong, honey?" Calix stepped in front of her and placed his gloved finger under her chin to tilt her head up to look at him. "Something's obviously bothering you."

She licked her bottom lip before sighing, and Calix dropped his hand. "I'm ready to get out of the treehouse and get some fresh air."

"Not sure how fresh the air will be after the horde has been passing through," Nathan commented, but Calix interrupted him.

"But?"

"But I don't want to leave because that means we will have to go back to the ranch," she explained in a whisper. Her brows furrowed together as she thought about it. "I know you said I could stay with you, but before the apocalypse, it was weird enough moving in with one new relationship after a couple of months. But now? Moving in with our three new relationships after only four days of knowing you? And the fact that I actually *want* to? How do I explain that to my parents and Spencer?"

"Hey, darlin', you don't have to decide right now. You know we want you here, but I don't think you'll be leaving. That was the biggest horde I've seen, and the last hordes we had did enough damage. I don't mean to make you upset, but I don't think the ranch will be livable like it was," I told her honestly, and the guys nodded their heads in agreement.

"Don't make a decision until we've seen the ranch, killer." Nathan grabbed her by the back of her neck and tugged her into him for a kiss. "We'll make this work no matter what."

"Thank you," she whispered, and we all shared a look.

She would be ours no matter what. Zombie apocalypse be damned.

14

TORI

A putrid odor poured into the treehouse the moment Nathan opened the door and stepped outside into the bitter cold air. I shivered, and I was glad I'd thrown on some leggings and a coat over Micah's flannel.

The dog still growled, but it wasn't nearly as ferocious sounding as it was before.

"That's a telltale sign of a horde coming through." Micah coughed a few times into his elbow as Calix paled and stepped outside.

My nose scrunched up as I walked out, and Micah shut the door behind us.

Cold seemed to permeate everything, and I shivered as we walked further out onto the deck. The treehouse had been chilly, but outside was freezing. Micah must've insulated the heck out of the house because the difference was clear.

"Five in the clearing," Nathan said, bringing his rifle to his shoulder.

Calix aimed his loaded crossbow, and the arrow went clear through the skull of one before he put it between his legs, stood on it, and pulled the string back to place his arrow, then brought it back up and shot another as Nathan shot the other three one after the other.

"Five down. Watch my back." Micah went to the edge of the treehouse and gripped the side before lowering himself down.

"Watch your feet as you come down, killer." Nathan lowered himself down after Micah, and Calix stayed up on the deck watching over them.

I dropped down to the pegs while holding the golf club and climbed down, following behind Nathan as he and Micah scoped out the area.

The frozen ground crunched underfoot, and the sun only warmed where it touched. "It's *so* cold. Do you think it's an early winter?"

"Probably," Nathan said with his teeth chattering.

"Or we just lost count of the seasons. It's been a while since we've had a calendar, I mean. I forgot the days a lot before the apocalypse." Micah shrugged. "Only difference was then I had a phone to tell me exactly what time of the year it was."

An arrow whizzed next to my head, and I froze before glancing up at Calix, who had his crossbow pointed behind me. I spun to my side to notice a fresher looking zombie hit the ground with the arrow still embedded in its skull.

I hadn't even heard it approaching.

Swallowing the lump in my throat, I glanced up at Calix and waved. "Thank you."

He nodded at me before reloading again.

"There's no sign of whatever made that noise last night," Micah said as he walked through the clearing. "Not any fur or massive amounts of fresh blood around."

"And it seems like we got the stragglers," Nathan added. "Thanks to Calix shooting that one."

"That's great. Can we check on the horses? I'm sure they're freaked out of their minds." I glanced over to notice Benjamin and a woman coming down from their treehouse.

"Of course, darlin'."

Just as we started toward the large shed, the other survivors started making their way into the clearing from their treehouses, including my family, and I had to ignore the disappointment snaking through me from being out of our bubble in the treehouse.

It was a *good* thing we had others with us, but anxiety spurred in my chest at having to explain our relationship to my parents.

There were two men and one woman that I

didn't recognize coming over from one treehouse, and I remembered Micah had mentioned there was a throuple in the group.

Excitement buzzed at having someone else with an unconventional relationship around.

They made it over the same time Benjamin and the woman with him did.

"How was it?" Benjamin asked me, shooting a look at Micah and Nathan. "I didn't realize until after the horde started trudging through that Calix may have had an issue with the additional roommate."

My face heated up as I smiled. "Calix is awesome. We did just fine."

"Just *fine*, she says," Nathan teased, reaching out and grabbing my hand before pulling me into his chest for a hug. "He's more than fine, and she fits in more than fine with us three."

Wrapping my arms around his waist, I leaned into him and nodded in agreement.

"I'm sensing something romantic here," the girl I didn't know yet teased with a smirk as her two guys pressed further into her, smashing her between them. "With *all* of you."

A snort came from Daisy as my group made it over. "Tori? With three men? She's never been that adventurous." The entire group shifted and looked at her, and she ran a hand through her hair. "I mean, she's usually kind of boring. Not that that's a *bad* thing."

"Shut up, Daisy," Spencer hissed before winking at me.

"While Tori was with us, we decided to explore the romantic connection we had," Nathan stated. "Meaning Tori's relationship with me, Micah, *and* Calix."

"Calix?" Benjamin's eyes widened before he looked up to where Calix stood on the porch of the treehouse.

"So it *was* a good idea to keep them separated," the woman with Benjamin murmured as she glanced at me with a nervous smile. "Hi. I'm Sally. I'm Benjamin's wife and Nathan's step-mom."

"I'm Ava." The woman standing with her two men smiled and swept her red hair out of her face. Even between the two large men, she was tall, coming up to their shoulders. "And these are my boyfriends." She pointed to the one on her left with dark brown hair and green eyes. "His name is Charles." She moved her finger to her right, pointing at the man with lighter brown hair, a beard, and brown eyes. "And this is Jack. I'm really excited to see another relationship like ours blooming."

"Tori. Nice to meet you all. I was planning on telling my parents a different way, but I am excited to see how this goes. The three of them are really sweet." I gave my parents a shy smile as Micah pulled me from Nathan into his arms and pressed a kiss to my temple.

Dad coughed, glancing around the clearing before leveling his gaze at Calix. "The one up there not want to introduce himself?"

"Calix is a germaphobe, hence the mask. He tries to avoid speaking to many people," Nathan told him, and Dad nodded before snapping his glower to Micah.

"Tori's a grown woman who can make her own decisions but do not hurt her."

"Never," Micah promised in sync with Nathan.

"Um, a germaphobe in the zombie apocalypse?" Jay asked, and the group seemed to shift their eyes to him, and he dropped it.

Dad cleared his throat before taking the moment to introduce everyone as he addressed the group as a whole, and then he let out a heavy sigh. "We appreciate you taking us in. I've never seen anything like what we saw through that window. There is no doubt in my mind you saved our lives, and we are grateful."

"You're more than welcome," Nathan told him.

"What was that god awful screech last night?" Mom ran a hand through her hair a couple of times as she glanced around. "I've never heard anything remotely like that before."

"Mountain lion probably got bit," Charles

stated, and a chill ran through me. "Something to watch out for since it probably turned."

"Um, can we check on the horses?" Spencer asked, rocking back and forth on her heels. "I'm sure they're terrified."

"Yeah. Let's head over. I noticed the sheds lasted through the horde for once. Which was a happy surprise. The hordes usually tear right through them, but Micah reinforced the structures with steel last year after one came through." Benjamin led the group to the large shed.

Soft whinnying of the horses started the moment Benjamin opened the lock and slowly opened the door.

Trigger, Dolly, and Belle peered out at us, eyes wide with fear.

We gave the three of them space, careful not to make any sudden movements that could startle them.

Trigger made his way to Spencer, and Dolly and Belle went to my parents. The three of them nudged their persons' hands with their noses, eager to see that they were there.

A pain spread through my chest as I watched them interact with their horses. I missed Kovu and his companionship, but most of all, it *hurt* to think of how he left this world. He had brought me so much joy and peace that no matter what had happened, I had thought we would face it together.

But in the end, I wasn't able to lift his spirits the way he had lifted mine all those years.

Nathan moved beside me and threaded his fingers through mine as Micah kept his hands on my hips, and I leaned into his warm chest.

They didn't say anything. They just provided the comfort they knew I needed.

"They barely ate anything," Jay said as he peered into the shed. "They drank some water, but not all of it."

"Probably because of stress," Dad explained, stroking Belle's nose with worry creased into his forehead. "We'll move the water buckets and grain outside and let them eat."

"Sounds good." Benjamin ran a hand down his face before clasping his hands together. "We didn't get to go over all the rules and what you should know when you arrived because of the horde. First thing to know is that we have Bane, Micah's dog who had been turned. He's become a sort of alarm for danger. If he's snarling and growling, it's time to either have a weapon or lock yourself up in the treehouse, *windows shut*. You heard the mountain lion. It should be no shock that there are things that can climb and still carry the virus or just do damage."

"Windows shut, got it," Spencer muttered, running her hands down her arms.

"Nathan." Benjamin nodded at him, and Nathan squeezed my hand before taking over.

"How to survive in the zombie apocalypse 101—if you hear some weird shit, *don't* go investigate it. Turn the other way and leave it be, but be cautious of the area you heard it. Your safety is never guaranteed." He glanced around the group as Bane made a low whine, and an arrow landed in the skull of another zombie near the trees. "Each treehouse has four exits. The smaller window at the top wall of the bathroom, the larger window in the living room, and the medium-sized window in one of the bedrooms. There are two ways to get down from the treehouse. The peg ladder and the rope ladder hooked to the railing that is constantly pulled up. Only use that ladder if necessary. It makes it easier for zombies, other survivors who don't know about the pegs since they're well concealed, or animals to get up."

"Once hope is lost, there is no chance of survival," Micah added gruffly. "We need to stay positive and look forward to the future. Set small goals and work toward them."

"That's a great point." Nathan squeezed my hand again. "I've drawn a few maps for each treehouse. There should be one hanging in the kitchen area of each one. It has the immediate area and a few other areas near us mapped out. I've marked the best kill spots, danger zones, hunting spots, and the river on them. If you're not good with direction, take it with you if you ever need to go anywhere."

"Another thing is that each treehouse has a small radio. Feel free to listen but never respond. The radios are all charged by solar, but we don't always know who else is listening and what their intentions are," Sally explained, fumbling with the zipper of her coat, and Benjamin zipped it for her.

"The seasons are changing faster than expected this year. Wood stove is the best source of heat, but only use it when you cannot stand the cold any longer during the day. Always turn it on at night. Nights get well below freezing," Benjamin explained before turning back to the group.

"All of that makes sense, but what happens now?" Spencer asked as she loved on Trigger.

"There was minimal damage to the Oasis even with the biggest horde yet passing through." Benjamin looked around the clearing, planting his hands on his hips. "I need to check the water tanks and the river. We should probably go hunting and have some fresh cooked meat for dinner so you're all up on energy. Then you can go check on that ranch of yours tomorrow morning. We'll build a coop and another shed for the horses for when you come back. Gives us something to do with all the treated lumber Micah has laying around."

"We're not sure if we'll be coming back, though," Dad mentioned hesitantly. "We are so grateful for your hospitality, but I don't think we're ready to leave our home unless we have no choice in the matter."

"Respectfully, Tom, you need to be realistic. Ava, Charles, and Jack lost their home last year to a horde. They barely made it out alive, and they lost Jack's brother in the heat of it. We're just trying to make sure you're not out there barely surviving. The ranch is probably destroyed. You know some zombies use brute force to go through windows. Sure, you'll be able to rebuild and clean up, but there will always be another horde. Are you telling me you're okay with having to do this every year or more when a horde comes through?"

Dad thinned his lips into a line and shook his head. "We'll think on it and decide after we see the ranch."

"That's fine." Benjamin nodded. "We're still going to build the structures, and you are more than welcome to become permanent residents in the Oasis if you decide to. Micah, can you help me find everything we need to make that happen while you're all gone at the ranch?"

"Sure." He pressed a kiss to the top of my head and followed Benjamin and Sally.

Ava, Charles, and Jack decided to go toward the supply shed to check on stock.

"Calix and I are going to go hunting. Want to

come?" Nathan kissed my cheek before pulling away.

"Yes, I do."

"We'll come get you before we go," he promised before heading back to the treehouse.

Spencer rushed over and locked her arm with mine. "Tell me all about the new developments, *sis*."

My face heated, but my lips tugged into a smile. "What about it?"

Daisy and Jay looked at me with pensive expressions, but I did my best to ignore them.

"Are you really dating all three men?" she asked, bouncing up and down.

"I am," I admitted. "And they're all really amazing."

"It's only been four days." Daisy snorted. "Are you really that—"

Jay slapped a hand over her mouth before frowning as he stared at me. "Not our business, Daisy."

"At least he gets it," Spencer sighed.

"Who do you like the most?" Mom crossed her arms as she shivered.

"I like them all the same."

"They're nice to you, right?" Dad ran a hand through his hair, and his brows pinched together.

"Extremely nice," I assured them. "I've never

liked someone as much as I like them. It's a weird feeling that I can't really explain."

"But you said you loved—" Daisy started, her voice muffled by Jay's hand.

"Daisy," Jay hissed. "Drop it. It doesn't matter."

She locked her eyes with his before sighing and nodding her head. "Fine, whatever."

"And it's not just because you've been locked away with them for a few days?" Mom checked, and I shook my head.

"I'm just happy you're smiling, honeybee." Dad ruffled my hair. "You've been depressed the past few years, and I figured it was the apocalypse. But you seem happier today than you have in years. It's good to see."

"Thanks, Dad." I beamed up at him, warmth filling me at the acceptance from my parents.

"Ready, killer?" Nathan strode over with Calix a few steps behind him, his eyes trained on me.

Spencer bounced forward, and Calix stepped back a couple of steps before I grabbed her arm.

"Germaphobe," I hissed in her ear, and she stepped back with a smile.

"Sorry. I just got excited. Tori's my sister, and I love her. I just wanted to meet the boyfriend of hers I haven't met."

Dad crossed his arms and stared at him. "I'm her dad, Tom, and this is her mom, Grace."

Calix nodded his head at them. "It's nice to meet you. Tori's very special."

Nathan tucked me under his arm with a grin. "We're going to go hunt while we can."

I waved bye to my family, and we left the clearing and went into the woods by a small path. The smell of rot still hung in the air, but it wasn't as potent as before. The ground still crunched underneath our feet, but it wasn't as frozen as it was this morning now that the sun had a chance to heat it up.

"Do you ever run out of ammo?" I asked, stepping over a log.

"We found crates of ammo for both the crossbow and my sniper rifle about a year ago, and we're not even halfway through it," Nathan said as we walked further away from the treehouses. "We only try to use it when we need it. We gather the arrows shot and soak them in bleach when we have enough of them, and Calix will reuse them that way. We do the same for Micah's longbow, but he prefers to axe things down."

Calix groaned, gripping his bow tighter. "Don't remind me of the state of the arrows before they were disinfected."

"Sorry, man. You know there are some good germs out there, right?"

"I know, but I can't get past the *germs* part." He made a disgusted face, and I giggled.

A snap of a limb sounded further down the trail, and a decaying deer stopped in the middle of it, staring at us with milky eyes.

A chill shot down my spine at the look of it, but before I could completely process what I was seeing, Nathan shot it between the eyes.

"Fuck," he muttered, sharing a dark look with Calix. "Hopefully there's some wildlife still around that's *not* infected. That was a huge horde. No telling how far it spread."

"There's not many places for animals to wait it out like we did either." Calix frowned.

"If there's a lack of animals, we'll just have to bring our livestock here with us. That's the plan anyway, right? We've been breeding rabbits for meat so we have those," I suggested as we moved around the dead deer and continued until we stopped abruptly, and Nathan raised his gun.

A smaller bear stood on its hind legs to the side of the trail, blinking with milky white eyes that made it clear it was infected, and Nathan's bullet embedded into its brain.

"Good idea, killer." He glanced around before tugging me off the trail a few feet with Calix. "We'll wait here and see what we can find passing through."

"Hopefully it won't be too long until something shows up," Calix sighed, glancing up at the trees. The sun made his green eyes look so bright outside, and he squinted them before bringing the crossbow up. "There. A non-infected squirrel."

"A squirrel isn't going to feed our group," Nathan muttered. "If anything, it'll just make the rest of us hungrier."

"A squirrel is better than nothing," he bit back, but before he could shoot it, it darted away. He groaned and shot an accusatory stare at Nathan.

Nathan held his hands up in defense. "Sorry."

Several branches breaking sounded up the trail before two deers rushed down it, one infected chasing a non-infected. The first deer's eyes widened before it ran, and the second had been missing an eye, and half of its face looked to be melted off as it hit another stage of decay.

My stomach churned at the sight.

"I'll take out the infected." Nathan brought up his gun and took the shot when it was a good distance away, shooting clear through the deer's skull, and the head seemed to explode from it—brain matter going everywhere.

Calix waited until the other deer was rushing past us before putting an arrow through the top of its chest, dropping the deer that hadn't seen it coming. He was a good shot with zombies, but to see how good he was with hunting deer was refreshing.

"Great shot, man!" Nathan grinned. "Can you go back and get Micah to help me carry it back?"

"Happily," he replied, reloading the crossbow and winking at me. "See you two in a few."

"Be safe," I murmured, and he nodded.

"You too, honey."

Calix headed back the way we came, and I stepped closer to Nathan, seeking his body warmth.

"I can help, you know. I handled the rabbit and cow meat on the farm with my dad."

His strong arms wrapped around me, shielding me from the bitter cold. "You're really something, killer."

"You think?" I hummed.

He pulled back before walking me back into a tree, hands on my hips as he guided me. "I know."

His blue eyes searched mine before he lowered his head and kissed me softly. His hand slipped under my shirt, and I jumped as his cold fingers glided up and down my waist as he slowly worked his lips on mine.

My hands fisted into his coat, pulling him closer.

A rustling sound broke us apart, and we snapped our heads toward the sound to see Micah with his arms crossed and an amused smirk pulling at his lips.

"Gotta be more careful out here, darlin'. Don't want anythin' sneaking up on you."

"My fault," Nathan claimed as we caught our breath, my heart drumming in my chest.

"Figured."

"I can help you guys carry the deer," I offered, and they both shook their heads.

"No need, killer." Nathan nudged my shoulder with his before he and Micah went over to the deer. "Let's gut it before we head back."

"We need to be quick to be able to have it in time for dinner." Micah pulled a hunter's knife out.

After they gutted the deer, we made our way back to the Oasis, and I couldn't be more grateful when I saw the treehouses come into sight. There was a large bonfire going in the middle of the clearing, and the warmth from it seemed to settle around it.

Calix stood beside it, warming up with everyone else, and I went to stand beside him. I was caught a little off guard when he moved to rest his shoulder against mine, and I smiled up at him.

"You okay?" he murmured, and I nodded.

"Just cold."

"Thankfully, Benjamin had the idea of the fire." He nodded toward Benjamin, who was talking with my dad on the other side of the fire.

Sally and my mom were also deep in conversation, while Spencer was over by the shed with Ava and her men, chatting away.

Micah and Nathan took the deer toward an old metal table they had out in the open, closer to the woods than anything else, and then they came back to warm up with us.

"It's fucking cold." Nathan rubbed his hands together near the flames. "Can't wait to get back in bed with you, killer. You'll warm us up, right?"

My face went hot with embarrassment, but I nodded. "Sure, handsome. I can do that."

He shot me a cheesy grin and wiggled his brows suggestively, making Calix clear his throat.

"Ugh," Daisy groaned, wrapping her arms tightly around Jay's waist and burying her face into his chest. "I just want to go home."

"We're heading out tomorrow," Jay reminded her, rubbing his hand up and down her back.

Daisy shot a glare my way before rolling her eyes. "I bet the house is just fine. It was silly to leave."

"Did you not see the horde come through?" Jay asked, disbelief leaking into his tone as he pulled back and looked down at her. "We should be grateful we weren't ground level with it."

"You know I didn't want to see them. It's morbid that you kept looking out at them anyway. It scares me." Her voice wobbled as she pouted her lips. "Besides, I need a shower so bad."

"We only have one shower, but we also have a river," Nathan told her.

"A river?" she practically sputtered, eyes going wide and mouth dropping in horror. "It's freezing!

Don't tell me you don't have a water heater for the shower?"

"Of course we do." Micah rolled his eyes, crossing his arms.

"Can we wash up soon?" I asked, glancing at Micah.

"I called dibs on the shower!" Daisy pushed.

"I'm fine with bathing in the river," I retorted with a blank stare, and she just scoffed at me.

"It's freezing."

"I'll take you. We can bathe together," Nathan offered with a heated stare as he dropped his gaze down my body and back with a smirk.

"You two don't pay enough attention to your surroundings when you're alone, so I'll come too," Micah said gruffly.

Calix snorted. "I might as well come too."

"You? Bathing in the river?" Nathan gaped at him before sliding his gaze to me. "You're already pushing yourself out of your comfort zone for her. I'm impressed."

"I can't have you three getting distracted. It's kill or be killed out here," he reasoned, and I giggled.

"I'm also fine with waiting for the shower. If that'll ease Calix's mind." I gripped my hand tightly to avoid reaching out and touching his shoulder like I wanted to do.

He tilted his head, and the tension behind his eyes eased. "Thanks, honey."

"Tori, wanna help prep the deer?" Dad called over.

"Sure!" I called back.

We dispersed from the fire, going to do small duties to keep the Oasis going. It was different from the duties we did every day at the ranch, and it lacked small luxury items we were used to, but somehow, it was even better.

15

CALIX

My gaze followed Tori as she glided around the clearing, interacting with Nathan, Micah, and her family. She got along well with everyone—well, everyone but Daisy. Even Jay had been respectful, but it was obvious that Daisy and Jay didn't fit in the way Tori and her family did here.

But what they did to Tori wasn't something that was forgiven easily.

Tori was different than anyone I had ever met. She had sparkling sapphire eyes that lit up when I talked to her. Nobody's eyes ever lit up the way hers did when I spoke, and they'd done it since the first moment I met her, even though I was rude.

My mother hadn't looked at me with anything except guarded eyes, but that was because of her phobia of germs. I grew up on avoiding germs like the plague—because germs *were the plague.*

I understood her fear, but getting to know the survivors in the Oasis and getting to know Tori had taught me that I didn't want to isolate myself the way I'd been doing my entire life. I just had to break the mindset…but I reacted without thinking most of the time. It was a gut-reaction for me to avoid most living and non-living things, but it was also unrealistic the way we lived now.

Tori made me *want* to change the way I saw things, but doing it was more than difficult. She was stunning, that was a given, but she was also intelligent and capable. I didn't even mind the fact that she'd helped skin and debone a deer.

I wanted to touch her anyway.

After she washed off, of course, but that fact was still insane to me.

The cold around us tried permeating the warmth the bonfire gave off, and we'd all begun to stand closer.

Ava and I were cooking the meat on two large rock slabs over the fire, and the sound of the meat searing made my stomach rumble.

It'd been so long since we'd had fresh meat.

"So, Tori," Ava started, glancing over to where she stood talking with her dad. "She's sweet."

"I like her. A lot." I shrugged, grabbing a pair of tongs and flipping the piece over. "I don't mind that Micah and Nathan are dating her too. We brought the idea up to her, and I was just happy she felt the same way we did."

She grinned wildly, grabbing the cooked meat to put on the plate and placing a new strip of meat on the slab. "It's so good to see you show interest in getting to know someone."

"It feels good," I admitted. My gaze wandered back to her, and I smiled behind my mask. "She's perfect for us."

We finished cooking the meat, and Tori, Nathan, and their dads went to wash up after cleaning up the mess of the deer prep and setting some meat aside to be frozen in the freezer that ran off the generator.

Tori popped up beside me and inhaled deeply. "Oh my God, this smells so good. It's been forever since I've had venison. We never hunted because we had rabbit and cow meat, which was great, but deer meat is so good." She glanced at me and Ava with a bright smile. "Thanks for cooking."

"Thanks for prepping." Ava waved her hand toward the metal table under the tree where they'd prepped the deer.

"More than happy to help!"

Everyone ended up gathered around the fire, plates full of deer meat and pickled vegetables as we talked amongst each other.

"Are you staying with the guys tonight?" Spencer asked after swallowing a bite.

"Yes." Her cheeks were pink from the cold, but they seemed to turn an even darker shade.

"Of course you are," Daisy muttered.

"Yeah. Of course I'm going to stay with my boyfriends. *How terrible,*" Tori remarked, shoving the last bite of food in her mouth with an eye roll.

I pressed my shoulder against hers, and she leaned into me with a sigh.

Dropping my lips to her ear, I whispered, "Are you okay?"

She turned her head and smiled at me, her face so close to mine it sent chills down my spine. "I'm fine."

The rest of dinner was uneventful. Bane had been relatively silent for the most part, and we didn't have any more stragglers come through.

Micah and Charles cleaned the dishes, and by the time they'd finished, the sun dipped below the trees, bringing a blanket of frigid air upon us.

The flames of the fire ceased, and smoke plumed from what was left of the wood.

"You should plan to leave at sunrise tomorrow morning," Benjamin said, glancing around the clearing. "Who is going to the ranch?"

"Our family," Tom stated. "Anyone else is welcome."

"We're going," Micah pointed to him and Nathan.

"I'll come," I said, and the group snapped their gazes my way.

"Are you sure?" Tori tilted her head, brows raising in concern. "You don't have to."

"I go on scavenging missions sometimes." I shrugged. "I'll be fine."

I wanted to see where she grew up, and it made me sick to think about her not making it back.

"Anyone else?" Benjamin let out visible breaths.

"I can come and help carry some things," Charles offered, scratching the top of his head.

"No need." Micah shook his head. "We need people to stay back too, and I'm sure you don't want to leave your wife."

He nodded, a grateful smile taking over his face. "Thanks."

"You have *two* husbands?" Daisy gasped at Ava, and everyone shifted on their feet.

"Yes." Ava smiled, glancing between her husbands with loving eyes. "We actually told you all that already."

"Oh." She frowned. "That's different."

"We were together before the apocalypse, and I would never change it. Even if it is considered different."

"Who cares if it's different? You're happy, and

that's what matters," Tori said, and Ava smiled her way.

Daisy went to laugh but covered her mouth with a fake cough.

"Something to say?" Spencer crossed her arms.

Her eyes slanted into a glare at Spencer. "It's just funny that Tori is saying that since she's seeing *three* different men. That's worse!"

"It's the end of the world, Daisy!" Tori exploded from beside me, her hands balled into shaking fists. "There's no need for your constant judgmental attitude anymore! You have done your fair share of actual *shitty things*, but you don't see me throwing it in your face!"

"Me? You're the one who dated Jay even when you *knew I liked him*!"

"Oh, shut up! You were screwing his cousin *and* his best friend!"

Daisy flinched back, and Jay's mouth dropped as he stared at her.

"Why did you say that?" she asked.

"Because it's true, and because you act like you've never done anything wrong. I'm sick and tired of you constantly putting me down when *I'm the one* who got fucked over."

"But—"

"That's enough," Micah barked. "We leave at sunrise. It'll be a two day trip there and back. See you all in the morning."

"But what about the shower?" Daisy piped again, and Benjamin interrupted before Micah could reply.

"It's too late. We need the generator for the hot water heater, and I need to refill the tank for the shower head. We haven't had enough rain lately. If you come back, it'll be ready then."

"I'll just take one at home then."

Tori's nostrils flared as Daisy rolled her eyes, but she stayed silent, simmering in her obvious anger as Micah pulled her to his side and started walking us back to the treehouse.

Spencer rushed over and hugged Tori, whispering something in her ear before shooting us a mischievous grin and bouncing away.

"Can you stay with us tonight?" Tori's tired eyes pleaded as she looked up at me, but a shiver racked my body.

"Not yet, honey. I'm closer, but…"

"I understand." The way she said it didn't sound like she was upset, but I was disappointed in myself for my inability to give her what she needed.

"We'll make sure she's okay," Micah promised, and Nathan nodded.

"It's okay not to be ready. You've lived the majority of your life alone. Needing time to adjust is normal."

I knew he was right, and I knew Tori understood. But it didn't lessen my desire to just be normal.

Ignorance was truly bliss. If I hadn't known about the complexity of germs and what could happen being exposed to certain things, I wouldn't live in fear like Mom had.

16

TORI

Dread settled in my gut like a lead ball that morning.

It was a feeling where I *knew* something bad would happen. I had it the morning I went to a golf game with Jay, and I got whacked in the head because I stood too close behind him when he was about to hit the ball. I even had it the morning that I failed a big agriculture test because of lack of sleep the two nights before. I also had it the day I caught Jay cheating on me with Daisy.

So when I woke up between Micah and Nathan, the warmth that spread through me quickly took a nosedive, and I hated that.

I didn't want the ranch to be destroyed, but the thought didn't destroy me either because it meant going back to the Oasis with my men.

We'd equipped our bags and weapons before

locking up the treehouse and heading down at the sign of first light.

Benjamin and Sally stood bundled up in the center of the clearing with my parents, Spencer, Jay, and Daisy.

The ground crunched with every step, and the breeze scraped over any exposed skin.

"Be safe out there." Benjamin and Sally hugged us before we went over to the horses.

Daisy stomped her feet as she walked over to me with her arms crossed tight across her chest. "I'm sorry," she gritted out before turning on her heels and going back to Jay's side before I could respond.

I blinked a few times, and I clamped my mouth shut. I didn't have to accept an apology when she clearly didn't mean it. Even if she did mean it, it wasn't my responsibility to accept an apology that I wasn't ready to.

"Woah," Spencer whispered, and Mom elbowed her.

"I'm glad things seem to be getting better. Steps in the right direction, at least," Dad said, fussing with the reins on Belle before letting Jay take over.

The horses let out a few visible breaths as they kicked at the hard ground.

"How are we going to do this with so many people?" Jay asked, placing the heavy blanket on Belle's back.

"That's why we don't have saddles," Mom explained. "We're going to be three to a horse."

"Who's riding with us?" Daisy asked, her wide gaze flicking to me.

"I am," Spencer groaned, crossing her arms. "Tori's riding with Mom and Dad, and Calix, Micah, and Nathan will be riding together."

Nathan pouted, planting his hands on my hips and tugging me forward for a kiss. "Ride safely."

"You too." My heart sank at the implication of his words. Riding a horse wasn't safe anymore. Not for the people riding or the horse itself. Not after what happened to Kovu.

"Return safely," Benjamin said as we got on the horses. I rode on the back, holding on to Mom.

Spencer, my godsend of a sister, held on to Daisy. I knew she did it so I didn't have to, and I loved her so dearly for that.

We left the Oasis with a blanket of unease over us. The overcast sky did nothing but make the ride dreary and cold as the sun took its time climbing higher.

The first couple of hours were uneventful aside from a couple of stragglers and the devastation left in the horde's wake. Smaller trees were broken down, jagged ends on the parts of the trunks left, and blood and chunks of flesh scattered the ground of the forest. The rotten scent lifted the further we went, but the smell of the air was still *off*.

Grief shredded my chest as we passed through the spot where we lost Kovu, and I held onto my mom a little tighter.

"His body's gone," I croaked, silent tears streaming down my cheeks as she patted my hands on her stomach. "How is it gone?"

"I don't know, sweetie. I don't know," she whispered.

I swallowed the hard lump in my throat as Dolly picked up her pace, trotting faster through the forest with the rest of the group.

"Stay alert. Watch your sides, back, and front," Micah said, his rough voice thundered throughout the forest. "Nathan's got his gun ready to take out any zombies we run across. If there's any smaller groups, get off the horses and kill them. We'll need more than just us. Sometimes after a large horde, zombies stick together in groups."

"That's not scary at all," Spencer huffed.

We were fortunate to go another hour further without interruption until a bloodied body of a man stumbled out of the forest along the path.

The dread I felt this morning amped up until all I could hear was static.

Just as Nathan raised his gun, the body threw its hands up. "Don't shoot! I'm not undead, and I wasn't bitten!"

Nathan didn't lower his gun, instead he had it

trained on his head. "And what're you doing out here alone?"

"I wasn't alone!" The man's face went red, and he started to shake. Blood caked his clothes and had dried smeared all over his skin. "I had a group I was with, but that damned horde came through and took 'em all! Can I come with you? What's one more person in a group your size, huh?"

"No," Nathan answered bluntly, and the guy shook more. "We don't know your story, and you're acting suspicious. I'm not chancing their safety for you."

"Nathan, the guy's clearly in shock," Jay started, but Micah turned his head toward him with a sharp look, and he shut his mouth.

"Yeah, *Nathan*, I'm in shock. Help me out. Don't leave me alone here to die." The man coughed, and I saw Calix flinch. "Man, you *know* how it is out here. Bein' alone will just get me killed."

"Not my problem." Nathan's jaw tightened, and he cocked his pistol.

"You have two choices," Micah said, his shoulders tense. "Get lost or get a bullet in your skull."

The guy had a gun pointed at his head, blood all over him, and yet he didn't act scared at all. It looked like he'd been beat up. His eyes were swollen, and he had cuts all over him. It made my skin crawl. Something *was* off with him, but I couldn't put my finger on it.

His lip curled into a snarl, and he spat on the ground next to Belle, and she huffed at him, swishing her tail in warning. "You're signin' my death sentence. Fuck you all." He glared at Nathan before slowly stepping to the side and walking back behind us.

Nathan turned, keeping the gun pointed at him until he was a good distance away, and then he uncocked the gun and put it in his holster. The horses started to trot again, and I glanced back to see the man staring at us with a glint of something dark in his eyes.

The dread didn't let up as we left him behind.

"Why didn't we take him in?" Spencer asked timidly.

"Yeah. That was fucked up, man," Jay agreed.

"I don't know. The guy looked weird." Daisy scrunched her nose, and for once, I agreed with her.

"Just because someone looks weird doesn't mean they shouldn't be helped," Mom muttered.

"Not at the risk of our family," Dad stated, and the group fell silent. "Something was off about that guy."

"He looked familiar," Nathan stated in a dangerously low tone. "The ticks he was doing suggested he had bad intentions. Body language doesn't lie."

"Familiar how?" Daisy asked.

"The only sketchy people I've come in contact

with like that were the ones who raided and forced Dad, Sally, and me from our homestead."

A chill ran down my spine as we continued on. Nobody brought the man who had stopped us up again, and I wanted to leave him behind us both literally and metaphorically.

But with the icky feeling in my veins, I didn't know if that would happen so easily.

We finally broke through the forest and into our pasture, and my stomach lurched.

The pasture had blood frozen over the ground, and the further we made it toward the house, the weight on my chest became heavier.

Nobody spoke a word as we approached, and even the horses didn't carry on with any antics.

The white paint siding was coated in bloodied hand prints and splatters. Grief washed over me, and it was so tangible I could feel my family's grief mirror my own. It was clear to me that our home that was once a safety bubble from the apocalypse had fallen into a disaster.

Windows were broken on the bottom floors, and the doors were banged open, even though we'd locked them before. Bones and flesh chunks were all over, and my stomach churned at the sight as we got off our horses.

The barn's door was wide open, and another wave of mourning slammed into me—but the coop looked to be locked up as tightly as we'd left it.

My feet were moving before my mind realized where I was headed. I gripped my golf club tightly. The crunching sound of frozen body parts were all I could hear as I ran to the barn. Spencer was beside me as we threw open the other door, and relief and confusion warred within me as we took in the state of the barn.

The cows mooed, and our bull, Blaze, paced restlessly in his stall. His hooves pounded against the hard dirt floor, and his nostrils flared. Blaze *never* acted so aggressively, and his gaze was locked on the cow laying in the dirt.

The stall door was open, and she had blood pooling around her head.

My gaze widened, and the dread that hung overhead hit me like a ton of bricks. Calix grabbed my arm to pull me back as Micah rushed toward the cow. His brows furrowed as he glanced up.

"The cow was shot in the head, and it's still warm."

Blaze let out a deafening roar and charged the stall door, but it didn't budge. It was only then that I realized he wasn't staring at the dead cow anymore. He was staring behind us.

Nathan pivoted on his heels, gun up and ready to fire.

"Put the gun down, boy," a creaky old voice sounded from behind us, and I turned to see an older man, older than my parents by at least ten years, with his large gun leveled on Nathan. "Fancy seein' you again."

Three other men came from behind him with guns trained on all of us, and my heart pounded against my ribs, causing a ringing to sound in my ears as fear clawed at my throat.

Calix held me so tight against his chest, and his arms wrapped around me. His heartbeat raced fast, and it thudded against my back as he held my trembling form.

The man from the trail stumbled from behind the rest of them with a wide grin, sweat dripping from his forehead and into his eyes. "You fuckers may not have fallen for my trap, but you fell into theirs."

"Shut up, Tommy," the old man barked, spittle flying from his mouth. "Didn't we send you off to die?"

"I tried helping you get some people like before. I proved my usefulness." He held his head up, chest puffed out.

The old man gave a rattled sigh before moving his gun over and shooting Tommy in the face then settled it back on Nathan.

All the blood in my body plummeted to my feet as Tommy's blood poured out of his head.

"He was bitten. Couldn't chance him turnin' could we?" The man took another step forward before tilting his head. "Any last words, boy?"

A whimper pulled from my throat as I trembled in Calix's arms, and the man's gaze locked on mine before he smiled, showing off rows of rotten teeth.

"Found another poor woman to sink your teeth into?" His slimy gaze slid back to Nathan as he raised a brow. "Does she know about what you did to my daughter? What you'll do to her?"

"What *I* did?" Nathan shook his head, still pointing the gun at him. "She's the one who gained my trust before betraying my family and me. Not the other way around."

"You slept with her!" he shouted, spit flying everywhere. "You slept with her, and now she's dead because *you* had to think with your dick!"

He turned the gun to me, and the men behind him leveled their guns on everyone else, including Nathan.

Staring at the end of a gun made my mind turn off, and it was a sort of out of body experience I wished I never had happen.

"You seem to like this one, but why is someone else holding her, eh?" His gun waved between Calix and me, but Calix didn't waver. He held onto me tighter than he ever had.

"Don't fucking hurt her," Nathan growled, and the man sneered.

"You knocked my daughter up, and she died because of it." He chuckled weakly. "It's only fair I kill someone you hold dear. Maybe I'll just kill both of them."

"That's *impossible!*" Nathan shouted, the hand holding his gun shaking. "I couldn't have gotten her pregnant. I didn't even come! She must've been with someone else!"

The man went tense before whirling the gun back to Nathan, walking up closer until the barrel rested against Nathan's forehead, and Nathan's gun butted up against his chest.

The men behind him moved their guns to Nathan only. They looked just as pissed off as the old man did, all but one. One looked jealous and guilty.

"Say that again," he dared as Micah's arms replaced Calix's, but I was too focused on the gun put to my boyfriend's head.

Fear paralyzed me to the spot, and I struggled to breathe.

"When did she die?" Nathan asked quietly, his chest heaving up and down.

"She died about a year ago." His lips curled in disgust.

"You raided our home over two years ago," Nathan said carefully. "The timeline doesn't match up. I couldn't have been the one to get her pregnant."

The man blinked before rage boiled beneath his already simmering murderous intent. "Shut up, you little shit! She wouldn't have had the chance to find another outsider without me knowing!"

"Maybe it isn't an outsider," Nathan retorted smugly before knocking his arm into the gun and tackling the old man. Both his and the man's guns flew to the ground, and their fists pounded into each other.

The men behind him couldn't get a clear shot since they were rolling in the dirt, and for that, I was grateful.

But the old man ended up getting the upper hand, and Nathan rolled on the ground, only a few feet from the bleeding, infected dead body in our barn. His boots kicked into Nathan's side before my vision pulsed red.

"Get off him!" I jerked out of Micah's grasp fast enough to swing my golf club into the back of the old man's head. It hit with a dull crack, and the man stumbled back.

Blood dripped down his head, and before he could grasp his bearings, an arrow shot through his skull, the tip sticking out of his eye socket before his body fell forward.

Nathan scrambled to his feet before grabbing his gun off the ground.

The men at the barn doors looked at each other before turning to run, but a third arrow shot through the heart of one, and another arrow hit through the chest of the other.

Micah slung his long bow back over his shoulder and pulled me against him.

Nathan lifted his gun and shot the last guy who had only made it a few yards away.

My knees wobbled, and I couldn't take my eyes off Nathan as he got back to his feet and winced before smiling at me with his busted lip.

"How did you three know how to get out of that situation?" Dad asked, his voice thick with fear and respect.

"The humans alive now are more dangerous than the zombies." Micah shrugged.

"What were they doing here?" Daisy's voice trembled. "Why did they kill the cow?"

"They're raiders. They've been following the horde and scavenging what survives it," Nathan explained bitterly. "They probably shot the cow for meat."

"She wasn't a meat cow. She was a milk cow," Dad muttered, and my chest throbbed. "Might as well take advantage of the situation though."

"I'll help," Nathan offered, and I frowned. "We just need to clear the house and coop first."

Nerves fluttered in my stomach. The ranch was a disaster from the horde, and I doubt we would've survived it. But I *knew* we wouldn't have survived the raiders that came through after.

17

TORI

The entire house had been ransacked aside from the upstairs, and my mom and Spencer were hard at work, putting things up and stuffing some things into boxes.

It was obvious the horde hadn't breached the house—the raiders did.

But even so, the thought of staying here again didn't feel *safe*.

Everyone else surprisingly felt the same way—including my dad. Since Benjamin planned to build structures for the livestock, we decided to bring all the animals with us.

We had a couple of trailers that could be pulled by the horses, so we planned to gather as much as we could and head back. It would be a harder journey with the cows, bull, and us walking along with the horses, but we didn't have much of a choice.

My main concern was the bitter cold with the animals, but as soon as we made it back to the Oasis, they would be warm again—and they were warm tonight.

Canned foods were stockpiled already, and we knew we'd have to use one of the trailers strictly for the chickens since we had so many of them. We would have to make a couple of trips to bring in some of the bigger supplies, but it would be worth it.

"Are you sure you're okay?" I fussed over Nathan at the kitchen table, ignoring how all the things were torn out of the cabinets and flung around. My hands moved around his body, pressing and prodding to make sure he wasn't more injured than he'd looked.

Nathan gripped my wrist and tugged me into his lap. "I'm fine, killer. Thanks to you bashing the old guy over the head with your golf club, Calix had a perfect shot to take him down."

My face heated, and I nodded. My body had acted on its own. All I knew was that I absolutely hated seeing Nathan being kicked while he was down—*literally*.

"I can't believe you hit a person with it," Spencer stated, shaking her head. "My sister is such a badass."

"She is." Micah strolled over and kissed my temple.

"Proud of you," Calix murmured, standing behind Nathan's chair.

"I'm not loving the whole three boyfriends thing." Dad groaned, running a hand down his face.

"Dad." I pouted my lips teasingly, but I honestly understood his discomfort. He hadn't even liked Jay, but he had been right about that one.

"No one is good enough for you, honeybee." He shrugged, sliding his gaze to Spencer. "Or for my peanut."

She frowned before grumbling under her breath about how the population had dwindled.

"We are up for that challenge, sir." Nathan winked at Dad.

"We'll do everything we can to be good enough for her," Calix added.

"She's already the center of our lives," Micah rasped.

"You better." Dad crossed his arms, looking every bit uncomfortable with the situation.

"Alright, well it's getting dark." Mom clapped her hands, dispersing the awkwardness in the air. "How are we going to do this?"

"I boarded up all the broken windows." Dad jerked his thumb to the kitchen window he had nailed a few boards over. "Enough of the solar panels are still working to run the heat tonight."

"And the shower?" Daisy's eyes lit up, but I winced as the memory of the well stacked with groaning decaying zombies flashed in my mind.

"Zombies piled up in the well somehow." Dad made a disgusted face that must've mirrored my own. "Do *not* use the water."

Calix cleared his throat. "Do you have water bottles?"

"We do." Mom opened the fridge and handed one to him, and I had been surprised to see everything was untouched in there. Maybe the raiders didn't think to check the fridge.

His eyes widened as he held it. "It's still cold."

"The electricity stayed on," she explained with a soft smile as Calix stepped away and carefully took the mask off to take a drink.

"I'm staying with you guys tonight," Spencer told my parents, rubbing her arms. "No way I'm staying alone in my room."

"We'll take our room," Jay said, wrapping an arm around Daisy.

"The guys can stay in mine," I murmured.

"We need to rotate watch tonight. Raiders or other zombies could be through," Nathan said.

"Daisy and I will take first shift," Jay offered, and Daisy frowned but didn't say anything.

"I can take second," I offered.

"Then it's settled." Micah scratched his beard and glanced around the room. "Everyone get rest while you can. We have an early morning ahead of us."

After saying goodnight, Daisy and Jay stayed in the kitchen while the rest of us went to our rooms to get some much needed sleep.

I paused at the doorway as Calix, Micah, and Nathan strode into my room and broke apart before looking around at everything. Flicking on the light to the room, amusement tugged my lips into a smile as I watched them. I understood Micah and Nathan, but even Calix was being nosy.

A sense of calmness settled over me as they walked around my spacious bedroom. There was a large window that overlooked the pasture, but the blinds were pulled down so we couldn't see the destruction of the land outside from the horde.

Nathan took a seat on my fluffy brown comforter, a perfect blanket to seek warmth in during the winter. I had to remember to bring it along. It would be so comfortable in Micah's bed. There was a collection of nude colored throw pillows and a throw blanket on the bed to add to the calmness of the space.

Calix stood at the small wooden desk in the corner of my room, surrounded by shelves filled with a few books and trinkets of horses and photo albums.

Micah was staring at the photos in the frames on the wall I had put up, something else I needed to bring with me to the Oasis. There were photos of my parents, Spencer, and me. One photo of Kovu and me after a horse show where he won first place, and it made my chest swell with mourning as Micah touched the frame of it. I had another photo of just Spencer and me up.

"Having fun?" I teased them, and they all glanced at me sheepishly.

Micah ran a hand down his face before coming toward me and pulling me into a hug. "Sorry, darlin'. It's interesting to see your space."

"No need to apologize. You're welcome to look around." I wrapped my arms around his neck as he picked me up and walked me toward the bed. My feet hit the plush rug, and I smiled up at him.

Nathan patted the bed as he stretched out and kicked his shoes and pants off. "Come on. This bed is *so* comfy."

I glanced at Calix as Micah got down to his boxers and got into bed. He had one of my photo albums and was thumbing through it. He was looking through the photos I had of Jay, Daisy, and me. Some of us together, some of just me and Jay, and some of just me and Daisy.

My heart dropped, and he glanced over with an unreadable expression. "Why're you looking at those?"

"Why do you still have them if they caused you so much pain?" he asked in a whisper, setting it down with the album open to a few photos of Jay and me before everything sucked.

"It reminds me of the past." I shrugged as he came and stood in front of me. "It doesn't cause me pain to look at it. It just validates my feelings of why I was so hurt."

"Your feelings are validated even without proof of the past, honey." He reached up and unhooked his mask before going over and hanging it on a knob for jewelry on my nightstand. "I'm going to sleep next to you tonight, but I need to be on this side."

My pulse raced, and I nodded wordlessly with my throat thick.

"Woah," Nathan muttered, slipping into the middle. "Dibs on the other side of her!"

I quickly peeled off my clothes until I was just in my shirt and panties.

Micah chuckled before taking the side beside Nathan and pulling me down to kiss my lips. "Night, darlin'."

"Night, Micah," I murmured before a squeal tore out of me as Nathan grabbed me and hoisted me up over him and Micah before settling me between him and where Calix would sleep. "A little warning next time!"

"Shhhh. Good night, killer. Thanks for saving

me again today." Nathan nuzzled his nose into my neck as I faced Calix.

"Good night, Nathan." I scooted my ass against his groin, making him groan as I made myself comfortable.

"Are you sure you're okay, honey?" Calix crawled into bed before laying his head beside mine and staring into my eyes.

"I'm okay. Are you? I know sharing a bed isn't something you want."

"Shockingly, I'm okay. I want to sleep next to you, Tori."

A smile spread on my lips before I let my eyes flutter close. "Night, Calix."

"Good night," he replied softly as I succumbed to sleep in my childhood bedroom with my three boyfriends.

"Tor, wake up," Jay whispered through the room, and my eyelids fluttered open to see him standing over the bed with a flashlight with an indecipherable look. "It's your watch."

Nathan grabbed me tighter by the waist and stuck his face in my neck, and Calix moved the covers up around my chest as he stared at Jay through tired eyes.

"I got it," Micah mumbled before getting up out of bed. "Go back to sleep."

Jay's gaze didn't leave mine as he shrugged. "As long as someone has the watch. It's been quiet so far, but it's necessary considering what happened."

"I'll handle it." He turned to Jay before gesturing for him to leave the room. "I'm letting her sleep a little longer."

I wanted to get up and go with him, but I guessed my body was too exhausted because I fell back asleep snuggled between Calix and Nathan.

My eyes jerked open, and I peeled myself from between Nathan and Calix before crawling down the bed and planting my feet on the plush carpet.

Glancing back, they were both snoring, limbs stretched out as they slept. I smiled softly, my chest swelling at the sight of them in my room, in my bed, and I grabbed my fluffy nude robe before wrapping it around myself and leaving the room.

The cold floorboards were a stark contrast to the heated air that I was so grateful for as I made my way downstairs and into the kitchen where Micah stood with his back to me.

His arms were crossed, and his posture tensed

with every passing second as he stared out of the window toward the barn.

"Micah, what's wrong?" I came around to him and glanced out the window before my throat tightened, and my body froze.

Out by the barn were two large bears with their flesh torn and fur matted as they made feral noises so faint from inside that I could only hear them if I focused on it. Their large paws clawed at the barn, making good-sized scratches in the wood as they tried to get inside as if they knew there were uninfected animals there.

"Oh my God," I gasped, pressing my hand to my throat. "How long have they been out there?"

"Only a couple of minutes. They just started going at the barn," he rasped, turning around sharply as he went for his longbow and grabbed a few arrows to hand to me. "Let's put them down."

I held them close and nodded, letting him lead the way to the door. He opened the door, then backed the bow, nocking an arrow before nodding to me, and I opened the screen door with a metal screech.

He lifted the bow and walked forward to the end of the porch and shot, hitting the closest bear through the head.

It dropped, and the second bear stopped scratching at the barn before sniffing the air and turning its face toward us. I rushed over and handed him another arrow, and he pulled back the bow and shot, barely missing the head as it jerked forward. The arrow embedded itself into the barn behind it, and fear rushed through my veins as it took off toward us.

"Arrow, now!" Micah shouted, and I handed it to him with a shaky hand.

He grabbed it, pulled it back, and waited until it came closer before he shot the bear in the head.

The bear landed near the bottom of the steps of the porch, and a breath of air wooshed out of my lungs as I handed Micah the last arrow he'd given me.

He pried my fingers off the plastic coated arrow before taking it and grabbing my hand, leading us back inside.

The warmth bathed us as we stepped in, making me realize just how freezing it was outside.

He let go of my hand to shut and lock the door, then he placed his bow and his arrow next to the door before hauling me up and walking over to sit me on the kitchen counter.

"Do you think the horde made the bears?" I spread my legs for him to step between and plant his rough hands on either side of my face. "I've never seen any infected animal on this ranch before."

"Yeah, darlin'. I think it was the horde. When hordes come through, especially of that size, they infect anything and everything they can in their path." His thumbs rubbed my cheeks before he slid one hand down around my throat and the other down to untie my robe and pull it apart.

"What if that noise woke someone up," I whimpered, his hand tightening around my throat before he tilted his head, hair falling in his eyes.

"I don't hear anyone moving. Besides, I need to feel you."

"You do?" My voice wobbled, but I did nothing else to stop him as he yanked my panties down my legs and let them hit the floor.

"Of course I do," he rasped as his hand slipped up my shirt and squeezed my breast, thumb flicking over the nipple and shooting tingles through me. "We're in the goddamned apocalypse, darlin'. And you're the first speck of happiness I've found since before it started."

"I feel the same," I moaned, my pussy throbbing with an ache that needed to be filled.

"Shhh. We don't want to wake anyone up." He tightened his grip even harder on my throat, but he was still careful with where he was squeezing, and he slid me to the edge of the counter and moved his hand to free his hard cock from his pants.

Nudging his blunt head against my soaked slit, he quirked his lips into a smirk before he tugged me closer. "Can you be quiet? Or should we wait until later?"

A whimper tore from my throat. "I can be quiet."

"Good girl." He gave a soft chuckle before he surged forward, entering me fully in one thrust as his lips descended on mine.

My body jerked at the sudden invasion before relaxing, and I wrapped my hands around his wrists as he kissed me passionately.

His mouth and mine moved in sync as I kept my legs spread for him, loving the feel of him inside of me, of him thrusting his cock into me over and over again as his hand stayed tight around my throat.

He broke the kiss, rolling his hips harder into me with a low moan.

My eyes rolled back into my head as I held onto his wrist for dear life, biting my lip hard enough for pain to ripple through it.

"You're being so good, darlin', so quiet." He quickened his pace, moving his hand from my throat up to where his fingers curled around the back of my neck and his thumb pushed down on my lip until it fell from between my teeth. "Don't hurt yourself." He plunged his thumb into my mouth.

I wrapped my lips around it and sucked as he fucked me harder and harder until he tensed, spilling into my heat as my orgasm crashed into me full force.

Sucking his thumb harder, I let out a throaty cry as pleasure rippled through me, clamping down on his throbbing cock as I came.

My heart pounded, and I could hear his too as he pulled his thumb out and we caught our breath.

He planted both of his hands on the counter, still inside of me, and leaned down to press a tender kiss to my lips before pulling away and grabbing a kitchen towel.

"Hope this is okay to use." He wiped himself before moving between my thighs to clean us up.

"It's fine. Just throw it in the bin so nobody uses it." I flinched as he wiped me down, tingles still shooting through my veins from the sensitivity.

He tucked himself back into his pants before helping me put my panties back on and closed my robe, tying it shut. "Let's go to bed, darlin'."

My eyelids drooped shut as I nodded. "Let's do that."

He picked me up and brought me back to bed before going to wake my dad for his watch.

And I fell back asleep without any worry, even of the infected wildlife that could be lurking on the ranch.

18

TORI

"Last night was quiet," Jay murmured before shoving a spoonful of eggs in his mouth.

I scoffed, and Dad raised his brows.

"Yeah, I noticed the two dead bears outside during my watch. Obviously it didn't stay quiet. What the heck happened?" Dad asked, grabbing his bottle of water and unscrewing the top.

Jay's eyes widened as he glanced outside, and his face paled. "They weren't there earlier in the night."

"Micah noticed them." I took a bite of eggs, chewing lazily before swallowing.

Micah finished his last bite before gulping a few mouthfuls of water and taking a slow breath. "They were trying to get into the barn, but Tori and I subdued them."

"What other animals should we be watching for?" Mom asked, wringing her hands together in front of her on the table.

"There could be…" Micah started listing some of the animals, but I couldn't focus on him because Daisy stormed into the kitchen and slapped her hands against the table, glaring directly at me.

"Why would you have the photo album out with photos of you and Jay? Telling your new boy toys a sob story to make them hate us?"

My mouth fell open as I dropped my fork on the plate with a clang. I glanced at Jay, and redness climbed up his neck as he ducked his head.

"Don't look at him, look at me," she snapped, and I turned to her and glared. "Don't act like Micah didn't pity you so much that he fucked you in the kitchen last night! I heard you guys!"

My body flushed with heat of embarrassment, and I blinked a few times as I registered what spewed out of her mouth. Daisy was always a bitch, but she wasn't always a bully. And she never used to hold so much hatred for me.

"You did *what* in the kitchen?" Mom whipped her head toward me in horror.

Dad's jaw clenched as he glared daggers at Micah. "Daisy, don't come in here and shout at my daughter."

"We killed the bears!" I defended our actions before narrowing my gaze at Daisy, my heart in my throat as I stared at a woman I used to call my best friend. "As for the photo album—"

"I opened it," Calix interrupted me in a cold tone, pushing his plate away as he placed his mask back on. "I pulled it off her shelf and asked her about it. There was *no* sob story. I didn't hate you before now, but the reason I do lies with you and not my girlfriend."

"Why were you being a total creep and listening to them anyway?" Spencer curled her lips into a sneer. "And to bring it up at the table? You're more of a bitch than I realized."

"*Spencer, Daisy, stop,*" Mom pleaded in a whisper.

"Daisy needs to stop causing issues with Tori," Dad stated, gaze locked on Micah's. "As for what happened last night, what if something had happened while you were distracted?"

"Don't forget she fucked Jay only a few days after meeting him," Daisy added in snidely, and anger flooded me so fast my vision dimmed. "Your sweet daughter isn't as innocent as you two would like to believe."

"I said stop!" Dad's voice shook with anger as he glowered at Daisy.

"*And you are?*" I shook my head in disbelief. "At least I'm not a backstabbing whore."

"Look who's talking. How many guys are you even having sex with right now?"

"Enough!" Mom's hands smacked the table so

My Rotten Love Life

hard it shook as she stood up, and her entire frame vibrated as she glared at everyone.

"Stop talking about my sex life. It's *none* of your business, Daisy," I seethed, trying to keep my tone calm but knowing my demeanor was anything but.

Daisy snickered, getting to her feet and crossing her arms. "Funny. You never used to have one with Jay. That's how we connected after all."

"And you said Tori was a whore? But now she's a prude?" Spencer snorted. "Make up your mind."

"Shut up!" Dad's voice boomed through the kitchen, and I jolted in my seat. "This is ridiculous!"

Micah grabbed my arm and helped me up as Nathan and Calix stood beside me as well. "This conversation is over. We're leaving," Micah declared, tugging me with them until we were outside.

"I can't believe your parents actually cared about the sex in the kitchen rather than the absolute shit Daisy said." Nathan scrunched his nose up.

"To be fair, her dad did try to shut the bitch up," Micah growled the words out.

Tears burned my eyes as I blinked rapidly. "God! That was *such* bullshit."

Micah pulled me into his arms and kissed my head. "It was. But it's unacceptable, and I'll make damn sure they know that."

"Are you okay?" Calix ran a hand through his

hair with a sigh. "I didn't mean to leave the album out."

"It's not your fault, man." Nathan shook his head. "They were clearly snooping in the room."

"And that's so weird," Calix muttered.

"Maybe they just noticed it." I sniffed and pulled back.

"Maybe." Nathan ducked down and pressed a kiss to my lips. "Either way, that was a shit show. What the hell is up with that girl?"

"I had a hysterectomy to take out my uterus a year before I found them together," I explained. "Endometriosis was hell for me, and I couldn't handle it anymore so my doctor tried everything else but eventually caved and gave me the surgery. It made my sex drive non-existent, and it took me a while to heal from it. I guess that's how she and Jay started their affair. I don't know."

"What a fucking dick," Nathan hissed as the screen door screeched open, and my parents and Spencer came out, Daisy and Jay following behind them.

"Let's gather everything up," Micah said gruffly, and everyone did just that.

The atmosphere was tense as we stepped around the decay and death around us, gathering supplies and fixing up the animals and trailers for the horses to carry.

It was a full hour of silent packing until we'd finally finished getting what we could that trip.

The chickens were loaded in a few large cages with blankets on the trailer Dolly pulled, and with them were all of the supplies needed for them and the cows. The second trailer pulled by Trigger was loaded up with household supplies and some sentimental items.

The cows and bull were following behind the trailers and horses, and we planned to have Daisy and Jay lead them behind the trailers while the guys, Spencer, and I walked behind them to make sure they didn't stray.

Mom stood facing the ranch with her arms wrapped around her center as tears flooded her eyes. "I'm going to miss our home."

Swallowing did nothing to ease the tightness in my throat as I nodded. "We won't be living there again."

"It's not safe anymore," Dad added, but the worry lines creasing his forehead showed how hard it was for him to leave.

"I'm glad we have somewhere safe to go." Spencer grabbed my hand and squeezed.

Dad turned and nodded at Micah and the guys. "I'm sorry for getting upset over you and Tori. It's just that she's my daughter, and you're new to her life. It's a weird feeling to treat her as an adult."

"She's been an adult for years," Nathan

muttered, and Micah elbowed him before clearing his throat.

"I understand the place of concern, but I only accept the apology on the grounds that you treat all of us as adults going forward."

Dad groaned before reaching his hand out and shaking Micah's. "Sounds good. I'm sorry, Tori."

"It's okay." I glanced back at the house again, and my chest filled with a bitter nostalgia.

I'd grown up in that house my entire life, and it was home in more ways than one. It was where I learned all of my firsts, and the fun times I had with my family and animals there were ingrained in my memories, even if we were no longer living there. I'd packed most of my room, but I purposefully left the album Daisy and Jay made a big deal about, only grabbing the framed photos on my wall.

"I promise we'll keep making trips until you have everything you need and want," Nathan murmured with a kiss on my cheek.

"Thank you for doing this for us." I turned toward him, and his lips met mine, sending tingles of comfort through me.

After a tearful goodbye to the ranch, my parents got on Belle to lead Trigger and Dolly with the trailers down the path back to the Oasis.

Daisy and Jay walked behind the trailers but ahead of the cattle, and the rest of us walked behind the group.

Spencer gripped my arm tightly as we walked away from our home, and I rested my hand on hers. The guys stayed behind us as we huddled together, and we didn't say anything for the first hour of the walk.

Spencer's grip loosened, and she turned to look at me with her brows furrowed together. "We're really not going back home, are we?"

"Not to live there anymore," I confirmed, and she nodded with a glassy sheen over her brown eyes.

"It's weird."

"It is, but at least we still have each other." I gave her what I hoped was a reassuring smile.

"Yeah. I'm glad." She glanced down as we walked over the cold ground, and the wind picked up, blowing chilly air around us until it seeped further into our clothes. "I'm sorry Mom got so hung up on the fact you and Micah had sex in the kitchen and totally spaced on what Daisy said to you until you left the room with the guys."

A weak chuckle left my lips, and I shook my head. "It's not your fault."

"She and Dad did go after her when you left the room. I don't think what she said to you actually sunk in until the initial shock wore off on them."

"What'd they say to her?"

"Told her she was ungrateful and disrespectful. They told her if she kept that up, she could stay at the ranch and take her chances with the zombies."

"Really?" My eyes widened, and Spencer grinned.

"Yep! As she deserved. She apologized, but I doubt she's sorry. I don't remember her being so hateful as kids."

"She wasn't." I glanced up and saw her holding Jay's hand and smiling up at him like she didn't just cause a lot of unnecessary drama. "I don't get it, but it's not really my problem, is it?"

"No. It's her problem." She glanced over her shoulder. "So, you slept with Micah?"

A genuine smile spread on my lips as I nodded. "I did. *Twice.*"

"What about Nathan and Calix?" she whispered.

"Nathan and I have been intimate, but we haven't had sex yet, and Calix and I have kissed," I told her, and my cheeks started to ache from smiling.

"It's so freaking good to see you smiling like that. I'm glad you found them, Tori."

"I am too."

A high-pitched shriek jolted us from our conversation as a small gray blur jumped from a nearby tree and onto one of the cows beside Daisy and Jay. Its head snapped toward Spencer and I, and its eyes glowed with an eerie yellow that made my heart drop into my stomach. Its fur was matted and disheveled, and its body was emaciated and rotten.

It snarled at us before opening its mouth and sinking its teeth into the cow's back. The cow bellowed, and the rest of the cattle scattered from the bitten cow—surprisingly, even the bull.

"No!" Spencer screamed.

The squirrel leapt from the back of the cow, claws ripping at the cow's skin before launching itself in the air, directly toward Daisy, whose face paled.

"Move!" Jay grabbed the bat he'd had and whacked it just before it landed on Daisy, and Daisy's screams echoed in the forest as she dropped to her knees.

Its body went toward the trailer with the chickens, and I rushed toward it just as it jumped on the trailer and reached toward the cages.

"Stay away from our chickens!" I tightened my grip on my golf club before swinging it back and hitting the squirrel's body with a thud, knocking it off the trailer. It hit the ground and rolled before staggering back up, the indent of the hit sunken into its gut.

My blood ran cold as I held the golf club up like a bat and readied myself for another attack.

"Tori, be careful!" Mom's voice shook.

Dad was coming toward me with another bat, but before he reached us, the squirrel hissed, digging its claws into the dirt.

It launched itself toward me, and I swung

again, but the squirrel's paws wrapped around the shaft, and its body swung with the club before it started to climb up it and toward me.

Fear slammed into me, and I swung the club at the ground a few times, but it just climbed higher.

"Don't move, Tori!" Micah's gruff voice demanded, and I froze.

The squirrel moved up the shaft, only inches from my fingers before Micah's axe hit its head, splitting his skull as its brains oozed out of it. He pulled his axe out, and its grip on the golf club ceased. The squirrel fell to the ground in front of me with a dull thump.

"It almost bit me!" Daisy sobbed, clutching Jay's shirt as he held her to his chest.

I sucked in a mouthful of rotten smelling cold air and dropped the club before hugging myself with trembling arms. "Oh, my God."

It had almost bitten me.

Nathan aimed his gun at the bitten cow and shot it between the eyes, and it fell to the ground hard. He put the gun back in his holster before he turned toward me and grabbed my shoulders, turning me to face him. "You can't throw yourself into danger like that without backup. We need to have a plan before we act."

"I…" My voice cracked, gaze straying toward the dead cow. "I didn't mean to. The chickens…"

"Can be replaced if needed," Micah finished.

"But I didn't mean for it to almost bite me."

Micah's eyes blazed with anger as he shook his head. "Of course you didn't! But it almost happened."

"Calm down," Dad said, walking up and checking me over. "She wasn't hurt, and that's what matters. You okay, honeybee?"

I nodded as Nathan let me go, but my body wouldn't stop shaking. It had been way too close of a call.

"You did good," Calix murmured, pulling me away from the dead squirrel and wrapping me in his arms. "You tried to protect everyone."

"You did," Micah agreed. "But from now on, wait until we've devised a plan."

"If you run in without saying anything, you can be a liability," Nathan added. "We just don't want you hurt, killer. It would kill us."

"Thank God you didn't get bit." Spencer went over to Dad and hugged him. "Can I ride with you and Mom?"

He nodded, leading Spencer away with Mom to gather the cattle that had spread out. "Let's make sure we have the cattle ready and accounted for first."

"It was so small. I've never had to fight any infected thing *so small*." My voice wouldn't stop shaking as I held onto Calix and inhaled his smell.

"It's a good thing insects are all wiped out. They

would've been the biggest threat." Micah scratched his beard.

A shiver shot down my spine, and I nodded. "That would've wiped the entire population out."

"This virus is doing a good job at that without the insects," Nathan muttered, running a hand through his already disheveled hair.

Once we managed to get all the cattle back together, we started our journey to the Oasis again, this time without any zombie squirrels or any other zombie animals. The only infected we ran into were a couple of stragglers on the path that were put down without incident.

It took longer to reach the Oasis than usual, and when we finally arrived, the sun had already started to set, and the cold temperatures had taken a nosedive into freezing.

Bane growled as we passed through, and his gums were rotting away, showing rows of barely hanging on teeth behind the muzzle. I grabbed hold of Micah's hand, and he gripped it tighter as we passed him.

Benjamin and Sally rushed over from where they were tending to the bonfire in the clearing, and my gaze widened as I took in all they'd done in preparation for us to come back. The Oasis had been amazing before, but now, there was a nice wooden chicken coop below where our treehouse was. There was also a new larger structure that was still being built, and it looked like a small barn for the animals.

My heart warmed at the effort they put in for us to be able to live comfortably here.

"Welcome back!" Benjamin said brightly, fixing his glasses on his nose.

"We weren't able to finish the barn," Sally said, gesturing to the half-finished structure. "Benjamin, myself, Ava, Charles, and Jack have spent every second available to work on it. The coop went up in a day, but we have maybe two or three more days to finish the barn up."

"We'll help," Micah offered, and Nathan nodded.

"I'm going to go change," Calix murmured before he made his way back to our treehouse.

My heart fluttered. *Our treehouse.* It sounded nice.

It didn't take long to get the animals settled. The horses went into the larger shed without much fight. Sally had moved the supplies into the smaller shed to give them more room. Ava, Spencer, Mom, and I let the chickens and the rooster claim their new coop, and they seemed very happy to be warm and snug in it. We'd brought the blankets and wood chips they had in their old coop along and made sure to make it comfy for them.

I wiped my hands on my leggings and grinned. "Looks like they're all ready for bed!"

"Stop it!" Ava groaned, shaking her leg, but it

did nothing to stop Randy from pecking at her foot. "Go do rooster things!"

Spencer and I giggled as Mom grabbed Randy up and placed him on his little throw blanket that seemed to settle him.

"Randy only does that when he likes someone," Mom explained with a chuckle.

"Pecking doesn't equate liking someone, Randy," she scolded our rooster with a waggle of her finger.

"He usually pecks Spencer," I told her, and Spencer's laughs grew louder.

"Thanks for the break!"

We locked up the coop, and we talked a bit more. Ava was so sweet, and she helped around the Oasis so much. It was obvious everyone here was a chosen family, and I loved it.

Calix walked up scratching his neck. The sun had fallen, and he held a candle within a silver candle holder. The flame's glow flickered on his face, and my chest tightened so hard it was difficult to breathe. "Want to come back to the treehouse with me?"

"Sure!" I loved the way my heart flipped every time he was near—every time any of them were near. "What're Micah and Nathan doing?"

"Micah's working on the barn with Benjamin, and Nathan's helping your dad with the cattle. They'll be in soon."

I smiled and glanced at Ava and Spencer. "See you tomorrow!"

"Have a good night," they called back as Calix and I walked toward the treehouse.

Once we were inside, I inhaled the woodsy scent lingering, and my body relaxed. It was weird how fast this treehouse became home for me.

"I'm honestly shocked that Daisy and Jay actually helped," Calix muttered as he stripped out of his coat, scarf, and shoes, and I did the same.

"I didn't think they'd pull their weight at first when it happened, but they've actually been doing a lot." I shrugged, and the cool air of the treehouse gave me goosebumps as I shivered. "It's better than the alternative though."

"I'll start the fire." Calix made his way toward the wood stove and started it up. "Hungry?"

"Starving," I admitted with a sheepish smile.

He grabbed a few cans of vegetables and put them in the pan over the wood stove. I stood next to him, soaking in the heat of the fire in a comfortable silence. Once the food was done, he left the pan on the counter with enough for Micah and Nathan when they came inside, and we ate standing next to the crackling fire.

"I used to play a lot of plague-type world simulation games, and while it didn't help my anxiety about how easily viruses and bacteria spread, it did give me hope that we'd have some sort of warning before it happened. There *wasn't* a warning with this. No extra deaths, strange symptoms, or increases in any illnesses. Just *zombies.*" He groaned, placing his empty bowl in the bin and putting his mask back on.

"I agree with that. There was no warning with the zombie virus." I finished my last few bites before doing the same, eyes locked on my usually closed-off boyfriend. I loved that he seemed to be opening up to me. It was a huge step forward from the bathroom incident. "Surprised was an understatement."

"Because of games like that and the media I fed into, my fear of germs was so high that I didn't have any real life friends. I had a few online friends and work acquaintances, but all of them thought I was weird since I refused to go out. It's difficult for me to get comfortable with people. I don't know why it's so easy to be around you, but I've even seen more of Micah and Nathan since you've come around," he admitted as we stood in the kitchen.

"I'm really happy to hear that, Calix. You can't help fear without controlled exposure, something you happened to be forced into, and I hate that for you. Screw the people who thought you were weird. They don't matter anymore, and for the record, it's easy for me to be around you too." I stepped closer, and my hand reached out toward him before I paused and pulled back.

His hand caught mine, and he pulled me closer.

"I've never wanted to *feel* someone the way I want to feel you."

"What do you mean?" My words were breathless, and my heart thumped wildly in my chest.

"I mean innocently. Hold your hand, skim my fingers over your cheek, sleep next to you, comfort you, and hug you. I've done most of that with you now, and it's been such a short time with us together. I've learned that time is even more fleeting now that we're in the apocalypse, so I don't want to prolong anything that I want or you want."

"Calix…" My brows furrowed as I stared at his determined gaze.

"I was never as bad as my mother when it came to germs, but you have me wondering if it's truly a phobia I have because I fear it or if it's something I've been conditioned to fear. Or perhaps it's just because I've adapted to the infected state of the world the way it is now." He used his other hand to take his mask off before bringing my hand to his mouth and kissing my palm. "But I also mean intimately in a way that isn't innocent. Ever since I walked in on you, Micah, and Nathan, I've been thinking about it. Knowing you and Micah were together last night doesn't disgust me at all. It makes me *want you more.*"

"I want you too." I swallowed hard and stepped closer, watching his body language for any sign of discomfort. My fingers slipped into his, and I squeezed his hand, feeling him tremble from the action. "I want anything you're comfortable with."

He leaned in and brushed his lips against mine. "Anything?"

"Anything."

"What if I want to try to have you completely, but I've never done it before, and I'm nervous about what it entails?" His voice shook as he pulled back and stared at me as if he were gauging my reaction.

I tiptoed up and kissed his lips again. "You can tie me up if you'd like. That way you'd be in control the entire time."

His eyes widened, and his mouth fell open. "You're serious?"

"Absolutely."

"Are you sure?" His brows bunched together. "You have no problem with that? Even if I don't know what to do?"

"It was my idea, Calix." I stepped back and let go of his hand before I went into Micah's room and came out with a rope he'd stored in his closet. "Where would you like to try it?"

"My room," he answered instantly, and my heart soared from the invitation into his sanctuary. He cleared his throat and went to his door before opening it and letting me inside.

Nerves fluttered about in my gut, and my heartbeat thumped loudly in my ears as I took a step inside.

As expected, his room was clean and organized. His metal framed bed was made with a tan comforter and white pillow, and he had a white nightstand beside the bed where sanitizer, a spray bottle full of what I bet was disinfectant, and extra gloves were set out. The floors were shining wood from being polished many times before, and the wood of his walls were just as polished.

A fresh, clean scent filled the room, and a smile spread over my lips as I glanced over at him and offered him the ropes. "This is really clean."

"Thanks." He swallowed audibly before taking the ropes. "How do we do this?"

"That depends." I carefully stripped out of my clothes, one piece of clothing at a time until I was completely naked. "Do you want me doggy or missionary?"

"Uh, *what?*" His gaze burned into my skin as he raked his eyes down the length of me and back. "What do you mean?"

"Do you want me on my hands and knees away from you or would you rather me on my back with my legs spread, facing you?" I explained, my legs squeezing in anticipation.

"That's what I thought you meant, but I didn't want to sound dumb," he murmured, reaching out and tucking a piece of my flyaway hair behind my ear. "The first one, I think?"

"And you're okay with me on your bed?" I paused before climbing up on it, and he nodded.

Once I was on my hands and knees, he came to the bed frame and tied the ropes to it tightly before tying my wrists together. It was tight, and the rope bit into my skin but not enough to make it hurt.

"Is that okay?" He pushed two fingers between the rope and my skin to make sure it wasn't too tight.

"Perfect," I assured him.

Calix stepped back and stripped from his clothes, and any air in my lungs whooshed out. He was slender with a good amount of muscles, but I had *no idea where he hid his cock*. It was thick and long with beautiful veins wrapping around it, and it was hard with pre-cum seeping from the slit.

My pussy throbbed in need for it, and I spread my legs wider as I arched my back more. "Calix, please," I whimpered.

"Please what?" His eyes widened as he wrapped his hand around it.

"Please touch me."

His face flushed as he nodded, and he reached out with his gloved hands and slid the latex down my exposed back, following the curve of my spine before moving them around to my breasts where he squeezed gently.

A moan fell from my throat, and pleasure vibrated through my body. The only thing that

My Rotten Love Life

would make it feel any better was if he removed the gloves. "Calix," I moaned again, encouraging him to keep going, but he pulled back.

"I need to really be able to feel you." The sound of rubber pulling hit my ears as he placed his gloves on the nightstand and came back, his hands molding over my breasts, and his palms skimming over my nipples as he explored them.

"Please!" I cried out. My pussy was dripping so bad, I felt wetness on my thighs, and I *needed him*. "Calix, will you please fuck me?"

He choked on a breath before his hands left again, and his bed shifted as he got on it. One hand gripped my hip, and he groaned. "Oh my God, honey, you're drenched. Is that all you?"

"Yes," I hissed, lowering my head and making my legs spread more for him.

"Did Micah come inside you?" he asked in a low tone, and I froze before glancing back, but I couldn't fully see him.

"Yes. He did. I didn't even think of that, Calix, I'm sorry. If you want to wait, I totally get it."

"I promise I want to do this," he assured me, but his hand left my hip.

"I get it. It's too hard to get around."

"No, honey, no it's not. This is for me, and I fully intend to take full advantage of this situation. *I want you, Tori.*" His hand splayed on my ass before his thumb spread me open more, and I felt the tip of his cock nudge through the opening until he pushed inside all the way until he bottomed out.

"Calix!" I moaned, and my body shook with ecstasy at the feeling of him filling me so completely.

He gasped, his other hand planting on my other hip, and his fingers dug into the flesh of my hips almost painfully. "This feels incredible. *Oh fuck*. You're so warm and wet, and you're squeezing me so tightly."

Pulling almost all the way out, he moaned before moving back in and stretching me for him. My pussy quivered around him as my own climax approached just from how truly *full and at his mercy* I was. He figured out his pace quickly, holding my hips for support as he bucked into me at a steady pace.

His moans mingled with mine in the room before stars exploded in the back of my head, and a scream tore out of me. Tremors shook my body as I slumped forward, but my arms stayed upright thanks to the rope, and Calix kept my ass up in the air as he continued fucking me.

He throbbed inside of me before his moans faded and his body tensed. "Tori," he murmured, giving a few more hard thrusts before his body trembled, and he stopped moving.

"Calix," I panted, trying to catch my breath as my heart pounded loudly.

I felt him pull out, and a squeak came from him before a loud bang echoed through the room with him falling off the bed.

"Calix? What's wrong? What happened?" I pulled at the ropes, but they bit into my wrists more.

His breathing became ragged, but he didn't reply.

I pushed off the bed with my knees and moved to the top of the bed where I was tied and looked over at him, and our cum flooded stickily down my legs. "What's wrong?"

"I'm so sorry." Calix was on his ass, staring at his dick with a nauseated face. "I wasn't expecting all those fluids to come out after we…"

"What happened?" Micah opened the door with Nathan behind him, and their gazes went from my wrists being tied up to his bed, to me, and to Calix. "Oh."

"Kinky," Nathan mused, crossing his arms with a smirk on his face.

Calix shoved up off the floor. "Don't say anything else, *please*." He rushed out of the room and locked himself in the bathroom without saying anything else.

Heat flushed through me, and I yanked my wrists again, but it did nothing. "Can someone untie me?"

"I don't know, killer. Should we untie you or take advantage of the situation?" Nathan strolled over and leaned his shoulder against the wall next to the nightstand.

"I got you, darlin'." Micah rolled his eyes and came over to untie me.

"Thanks." I let out a breath of relief as I rubbed the raw marks on my wrists. "Is he okay?"

The door to the bathroom slammed open before his footsteps echoed his fast pace until he came back in. "I'm so sorry, honey. I forgot to untie you and left you on the bed. All because I couldn't handle the fluids."

"It's okay, Calix, I promise." Micah pulled his flannel off before placing it over my shoulders, and I put it on. "I should've told you that it'd be messy."

"I should've *known* that. I was just excited. I'm sorry."

"Don't be," I assured him as I got up and wrapped my arms around his waist gently. "I understand."

"Thank you, Tori." He cupped my face and pulled me back until his lips sealed over mine.

Micah and Nathan shared a look before smiling at us, and my heart fluttered with the fact that I'd finally been intimate with Calix. We'd bonded tonight in a way I hadn't expected us to in a while, and I felt so much closer to him.

19

MICAH

Tori coming into our life wasn't expected, but her and her family coming to the Oasis was a blessing for more than just us in this last month. The contributions of their farm animals and extra hands and supplies came in handy. Miraculously, even Daisy and Jay did their part, even if their presence annoyed us because of what they did to Tori, and Daisy's attitude toward our woman pissed us off. But she'd stayed away for the most part.

Calix had come so far after being intimate with Tori. He'd even stopped wearing his mask around the treehouse with us, which was a huge step. He and Tori have had sex a couple of more times since the first time, and the last, he'd done it in missionary. Nathan couldn't stop teasing him though, which Tori and I found all the more amusing.

Nathan's dad and Sally went with Tori's parents for another supply run at their ranch twice in a row and finished bringing everything of importance over for the winter. The only supplies we needed more of were medical supplies, just in case we needed them through the winter.

Winter dropped below freezing most of the season, and snow piled heavy to the point where we had to hunker down at the Oasis and not travel out, so we wanted to make sure we had all the supplies we could possibly have before the first snowfall.

Tori's naked body shivered as she undressed in the wooden shed that served as our shower, and her nipples pebbled as goosebumps covered her skin. "So cold." Her teeth chattered as Nathan started the water, and she yelped as the icy water hit our skin.

"Come here, honey." Calix wrapped his arms around her as she turned into him for warmth.

It was only Calix's second shower with all of us together, and it was a good thing. Tori liked it when we were all together. It was one of the sweetest things.

I glanced over near our towels that were on top of our clothes on the sink next to the door as a ripple of cold jolted through me. It was early morning, but we liked getting clean before everyone woke up.

Nathan grabbed the soap and lathered himself

up before doing the same to Tori, and she leaned against Calix's chest as both of their hands soaped her body. I squirted the shampoo in my hand before putting it in her hair and washing it until the suds were covering her head.

Something about just taking care of this woman made us feel complete, and I was grateful that it was them she wanted with us. I loved everything about the dynamic we had together.

The water finally heated up, and we moved her under the warm stream to rinse her off before a knock sounded on the door.

"In a minute!" I called back, but there was another more persistent series of knocks without a reply.

We finished rinsing off before we grabbed the towels, but the knocks were so persistent it shook the door.

"What could've happened?" Tori murmured, shaking from either fear or the cold.

I swung the door open with adrenaline pumping through me to reveal Daisy's hand still up in the knocking position and Jay standing next to her with a sheepish look.

"What's going on?" I asked gruffly, irritation flaring through me.

"Nothing, man, we're sorry. She thought someone left it on." Jay ran a hand through his hair and stepped back.

"Um, *no.*" Daisy huffed, crossing her arms before glaring at the four of us. "Other people want showers too, you know."

"Yeah. Which is why we take ours before the sun rises," Nathan retorted.

"Together?" She twisted her lips to the side.

"Yup." Nathan wrapped his arm around Tori. "Got a problem with that?"

Daisy shook her head slowly before frowning at Tori. "Wow. You're actually fucking all three of them together, then? You were too self-absorbed to show Jay the attention he deserved because you *lacked a sex life*, but you're fine with whoring yourself out to three men."

"Daisy, stop." Jay grabbed her hand, but she shook him off.

"No. It's bullshit, and you said it yourself!"

"I am *not* a whore!" Tori seethed, visibly shaking in Nathan's embrace, and anger flooded me.

"Yeah. Like your year-long *dry spell* because of the surgery *you chose to get* just magically healed itself when three cocks were in front of you." She snorted. "Jay always deserved better than a closet whore."

Tori's face turned a shade of red before she jerked out of Nathan's arms and stomped between Calix and I. She pulled her arm back with a closed fist and threw a punch in Daisy's face with a resounding crack. "*I'm not a whore,* and I was the one who deserved better than both you and Jay. And I did better with the men I'm dating now."

Daisy's eyes watered immediately, and her head flew back before she held her nose that already had a trickle of blood running out of her nostrils. "Did you just *punch* me?"

I pulled Tori back and stepped in front of her before glaring down at the bitch as I noticed two shambling bodies enter the clearing. "If it were me, I would've done more than just *punch* you. Watch your mouth around her."

Jay grabbed Daisy's arm and tried to pull her back, but she kept shaking him off. "I'm sorry on her behalf."

"What?" Daisy spun in place before pointing her finger in his face. "You were just agreeing with me that it was *gross that she was with them all*!"

He winced before shaking his head. "It's not our business."

Two gunshots rang out, and the two jumped before Benjamin walked up with his gun in his hand as he approached them. "I am frankly disgusted by you two. Interrupting them in the shower was bad enough, but going off on Tori the way you did was disrespectful, and Micah was right. If it were me, I'd feel like you were a danger to our home. I don't know if you've realized the way the world is now, but causing issues with other survivors suggests that you enjoy sowing seeds of discord."

"But she—"

He held his finger to his mouth, cutting Daisy off before continuing. "I have no problem sending you two on your own if I see another display of *bullying* in the Oasis. We don't tolerate that here."

"We understand." Jay went white as a sheet as he tugged on Daisy to leave the shower with him.

Benjamin turned toward us. "Do you feel they should leave?"

Tori shook her head, but the guys and I stayed silent. "I don't want to be responsible for that."

"You wouldn't be. I would." Benjamin shrugged and spun on his heels to face them again. "One more issue with you harassing others, you're gone."

Tears flooded Daisy's cheeks as she finally let Jay pull her away from us.

"You four get dressed. You don't need that kind of shit." Benjamin nodded at his son, and I shut the door.

Tori let out a steady breath as she dropped her towel and cupped her mouth. "Oh shit. I punched her."

"You stood up for yourself, killer." Nathan kissed her cheek before grabbing her clothes and handing them to her.

After we were all dressed, she hesitated at the door before facing us. "Daisy wasn't always such a bitch. She used to be my best friend. We spent all the time in the world together growing up, and we did all the normal things best friends did together. Spencer and I thought of her as another sister. But she was always a little boy crazy. She was obsessed with this group of guys in college, and the one she was least interested in asked me out. That was Jay. After we started dating, she acted differently. Always made herself out like she was better than me. It was weird, but I never thought she'd turn out like *this*."

"Jealousy makes people do crazy things," Calix murmured.

"It's also not your fault, darlin'." I leaned down and kissed her head. "Let's go see what we can do to prepare for our supply trip."

When we got out into the clearing, the sun was starting to peer over the horizon, and the temperature wasn't as cold as it had been earlier that week. Spencer grabbed Tori the moment we'd left the shed, and she gave us a small smile before hurrying off with her sister.

"We need to make that supply run soon," Nathan mentioned as we headed toward his dad.

"Yeah. The lack of meat in the area is too concerning." Calix adjusted his mask on his face. He'd been doing great with coming around the other survivors in the Oasis as well, just with his mask on.

"No kidding," I muttered and ran a hand down my face. "We need to plan to go while the weather's like this."

"Tomorrow?" Nathan yawned as we reached his dad, Sally, and Tori's parents.

"For a supply run?" Benjamin quirked a brow, and Nathan nodded. "Perfect. We were just talking about how low our medical supplies are."

The rest of the morning was spent getting everything ready for the supply run. We'd done it what felt like a million times, but for some reason knowing Tori would be with us spurred a new kind of anxiety in my gut.

20

NATHAN

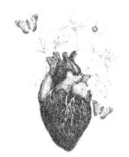

It was still afternoon as we passed Daisy and Jay in a heated argument below their treehouse, and Tori paused for a moment.

"You don't get it! I need something! I can't just free bleed everywhere!" Daisy shouted, waving her arms like a crazy person.

"Why can't we just ask—"

"It's not something you can just ask for!"

Tori took a deep breath and changed directions to head over toward them, and I held my breath as I kept her pace. "Excuse me, but if it's about your period—"

"What could you possibly know about a period? You don't even *have one anymore!*"

Did this bitch ever learn?

"Daisy!" Jay shouted loudly, and she slammed her mouth closed but kept glaring daggers at Tori.

Tori just rolled her eyes. "Suffer then." She turned and kept our path toward the woods, and I followed behind her. "See if I try to help you again."

"Wait," Jay called after us. "Is there anything we can use?"

"Pads and tampons are in the supply shed. Good for more than just menstrual bleeding," I hollered back without turning my head, and Tori and I kept going toward the forest.

I could hear Daisy throwing another fit, but I didn't care to listen anymore.

"Sheesh." I shook my head. "Almost a shame Dad didn't hear her say that to you."

She just shrugged with that pensive look on her face that she'd had since she finished talking to Spencer that morning. "Think we'll find anything?"

"Honestly?" I adjusted my sniper rifle on my shoulder. "Nope. But alone time with my girlfriend is enough to make me happy."

She let out a small laugh before I wrapped my arm around her shoulders. I loved the way she snuggled closer with one hand lazily gripping her golf club. "Me too."

There wasn't anything about Tori that I didn't love.

We made our way to the smaller clearing about ten minutes away and set up a spot with a blanket under us to watch for anything. Tori's knees tucked under her as she made herself comfy but alert enough to look for anything to hunt. Her golf club and my gun laid beside us.

I didn't want to hold my breath on finding anything. The last horde that went through seemed to really fuck up the wildlife. Strangely enough, we didn't run into a single animal on the way here—even an infected one.

"What's on your mind, killer?" I leaned back on the blanket and crossed my arms behind my head to stare up at her. "You've been quiet ever since you and Spencer talked earlier."

"We just went through everything Daisy has done through the years," she muttered, running a hand through her pretty brown hair with a sigh. "I just don't get why she always throws the surgery in my face with Jay. She supported me getting the surgery because she saw firsthand how much suffering I did two weeks out of the month. Now she's saying I chose it. It was my only option at that point, and I didn't take the decision lightly."

"I'm happy you're not in pain like that anymore. I think Daisy's just manipulative and delusional." A gust of cool wind blew through, and she shivered. I reached out and grabbed her arm before tugging her down on top of me.

"Yeah. I know." She rested her hands on my

chest and pushed up before straddling my waist. "It's extra quiet today," she murmured as her gaze heated.

"It is," I agreed, smirking at her. "What would you like to do while we wait for something to come by?"

"I can think of something." Her fingers worked at my belt before unzipping my pants.

Desire spread through me, and my cock throbbed as she pulled it out, her slender fingers wrapping around the base. "Yeah? What's that?"

"I was thinking I could ride you." She let go of me long enough to shimmy out of her leggings, panties, and shoes.

My heart damn near froze. We hadn't had the chance to have sex together yet. I'd wanted to wait to be with her the first time when we were alone, and this had been the first time we had been alone.

"You're seriously a dream, killer." I pulled my jeans down around my thighs to give her more room to work.

"You're a dream for me too, handsome." She straddled me again, gripping my cock and guiding me into her warmth before letting go and pushing further down on me until she rippled around me with a sultry moan. Her eyelids fluttered shut, and her lips parted as she started moving. "Ah, *Nathan*."

"Fuck," I moaned, and her desire and mine

worked together. I went to grab her hips, but she swatted them off.

"No. I'm the one fucking you right now." She rotated her hips as she moved, and pleasure zapped through me as I watched her use me to fuck herself until her eyes rolled back. "Lay back and let me do this."

"Can't argue with that." I slipped my hands up her sweater, grabbing her breasts and playing with her nipples, loving the way her pussy tightened around me with each tweak I gave them. "You're so perfect."

Tori's moans filled the forest, and mine followed along behind her as she bounced up and down on my cock, filling herself over and over again until her body stiffened. At the same time, a branch cracked on the other side of the clearing, and we both glanced over to see a zombie shambling toward us, dragging one broken leg behind himself. It was in the final stages of decay, and it moved *so slow*.

"Nathan…" Her pussy squeezed me so tight.

"We can finish, killer." My hands fell to her waist, and this time she didn't stop me as I bucked up into her roughly, chasing the feeling tearing through me with abandon. Every second, it came closer, but the adrenaline poured through my body, coaxing my orgasm.

"Yes! Nathan, right there, don't stop! Please don't stop," she cried out, her walls continuing to spasm around my cock until I came inside of her with a louder moan.

I thrust a few more times as my body and mind buzzed with pleasure, and her shoulders slumped. She leaned down and kissed my lips before we turned and noticed the zombie was now three quarters of the way toward us.

She jumped off me, and my cock hit my stomach with a wet slap as she stumbled off the blanket and fell into the bush next to us with a yelp. "Ouch!"

"You okay?" My gaze widened as the zombie sped up. "Shit." I grabbed her golf club and rushed forward as I swung it, bashing its skull to pieces as it dropped back onto the ground with a disgusting thump. The blood and brain matter splattered the ground, just before the blanket, and thankfully none of it got on me.

I shivered. I *hated* fighting zombies, but apparently, I hated fighting them naked even more. Glancing down at my dick, I was relieved to see it was uninjured.

"Um… I'm stuck," she whined, and I heard the cracking of branches as she tried to get up.

I dropped the golf club before turning to Tori, who had fallen right into the tangle of branches. The arm of her sweater soaked up blood, and there was a large slash down the fabric from a sharp branch she must've caught when she fell.

"Fuck, killer." I rushed over to her and knelt down, carefully untangling the branches from around her naked legs and hips, careful not to scrape her any worse than she already was.

"It actually really hurts." She grabbed my arms as I helped hoist her up out of the bush and onto the blanket. "*Shit.*"

I peeled back where the fabric had torn to see the deep gash of her arm and winced. It was deep, but it probably didn't need stitches. "It's a good cut. We need to wrap it and head back." I turned and grabbed her panties, helping her slide them up her legs before grabbing her leggings and doing the same.

"Thank you." She stepped back into her shoes with my help, and we frowned at each other before laughter bubbled out of both of us.

"I can't believe that happened!" I chuckled, tearing her sweater where it was already cut and making the fabric a make-shift bandage as I wrapped it around the five inch gash in her arm. "I mean, you rode my cock in front of a *zombie*."

"Oh, man." She giggled, wincing slightly as I tied it over the wound. "We really did that."

"We did." Warmth spread through me at the fact that this woman was actually mine. "Let's get you back and clean that."

A rustling sounded from above us, and I

grabbed her and pulled her closer as I reached down and got my gun.

I slowly glanced up, and my heart plummeted as I locked gazes with dead eyes. Up in the tree above us was a matted and undead mountain lion. "Don't move."

Her entire body was stiff as I maintained eye contact with it and raised my gun.

It let out a low, choppy growl, baring its teeth before lunging forward and landing on the remnants of the earlier zombie. It glanced back at us, and I made sure the gun followed it. It darted away from us in the opposite direction of the Oasis as I pulled the trigger. The bullet hit its shoulder, and it roared but continued running away from us.

"It has to be the one we heard go down during the horde," I told her, and she swayed into me. "Tori?"

She sucked in a stuttered breath before squeezing her eyes tight. "I'm dizzy, and I think we may have just died. How long was it there?"

"I don't know." I bit down on my lip before slinging my gun over my shoulder and grabbed her golf club and the blanket before we started back toward home. "But I don't like how close of a call that was."

"Me either," she mumbled. "But the sex was still great."

"Yeah. Life-threatening sex really makes our sex-life exciting."

She giggled, but I wasn't actually joking. It was great even if we did almost die.

We made it to the treehouse without running into anyone, and Tori immediately started stripping when we shut the door.

"What happened?" Micah's gruff voice was immediate as he came from his bedroom.

Tori winced as I helped her pull the sweater off. "I fell into a bush."

"You *fell?*" He arched a brow. "And cut your arm?"

"We had sex in front of a zombie, and she hopped off me as soon as it came close and stumbled into a bush," I clarified.

Micah's lip twitched like he was holding back a smile, but he shook his head. "You two have to be more careful."

"We didn't mean for that to happen." Tori shimmied out of her leggings and yelped as she bumped her arm on the wall. "Shit. I got blood on the wall. Calix is going to lose it."

"I'll clean it, darlin'. You go clean the wound."

"Blood?" Calix rushed from his room and paused as he took in Tori's disheveled state and the blood. "What happened? Tell me you didn't get bit." His voice cracked, and my heart ached from his words.

"No! No. I didn't get bit. A branch cut my arm when I fell into a bush," she explained. "But I'll keep blood off everything. So don't worry."

Relief flooded his features before he moved forward and wrapped his fingers around her wrist, pulling her into the bathroom with him. "You need to disinfect it now, honey. Let me help you clean it. I know how to prevent infection."

Micah and I shared a surprised look. Calix had really come so far, and it was all thanks to Tori.

"Listen…the zombie wasn't the only issue we ran into," I told Micah, and his shoulders stiffened. "We saw a zombie mountain lion, and it could've been watching us for a while in a tree above us. It didn't try to bite us though, it ran away, and I shot it in the shoulder as it did. It went away from the Oasis, but it's definitely posing a danger."

"And you're sure it was a zombie?"

"Definitely." I swallowed hard, and his frown deepened. "I'm going to go tell Dad and the rest of the survivors, so they know to bring a weapon at all times, no matter where they go."

"Good." He nodded, glancing back at the bathroom. I swore I saw a flicker of fear go through him.

"Go help Calix. He may need assistance," I murmured. "I'll be back soon."

Micah nodded. "Be careful." He started toward the bathroom without another word as I left the treehouse to inform the Oasis about the looming danger.

I'd hoped the zombies weren't evolving further. That mountain lion was too intelligent for my liking, but maybe it was some freak of nature and not something to be worried about.

21

TORI

Nathan came back into the treehouse soaking wet from the rain that started to pour down. He stripped as soon as the door slammed shut behind him.

Rain pounded against the roof, and the sound thudded with a calming rhythm.

"I'll start the fire," Calix murmured, kissing my temple as he got up and went to the wood stove.

He'd bandaged my arm tight and cleaned and disinfected it so well that I wasn't worried about any infection happening. Thankfully, it wasn't as deep as it looked in the woods. It just bled a lot for some reason.

Thinking back to our time in the woods earlier, my body flushed with heat. It was worth the pain.

"Dad has issued new rules in light of the infected mountain lion roaming around. Doors and windows must be closed and locked at all times. Keep a curtain over any windows, and don't go out alone. We're implementing a buddy system," Nathan told us as Micah passed him new clothes to put on.

Micah came back with a sheet and duct tape to tape over the window, and I got up off the couch and went over with the guys to peer out.

The sky had darkened considerably even though it wasn't sunset yet, and sheets of rain seemed to stretch on forever, blurring our vision of outside. Raindrops raced down the window, each streak coming together to form a waterfall as the wind blew the rain into us.

A pit of dread swelled in my gut as Micah and Nathan taped the sheet to the window while Calix covered the rest. "To be honest, it feels like something bad's going to happen."

"What do you mean, darlin'?" Micah finished securing the sheet before turning back to me.

"I don't know how to explain it."

"We'll be extra careful then, killer. It's all we can do, and we had a rough day." Nathan tilted his head and handed the duct tape back to Micah.

"I'll double check the treehouse though." Micah immediately started checking all entrances and exits before assuring me everything was okay.

We managed to eat a small dinner before heading into Micah's bed, and before Calix could turn toward his bedroom, my hand grabbed his wrist and tugged.

"I need you all with me tonight."

His eyes softened as he smiled and nodded, blowing out the candles in the living room and following us into Micah's room.

Once we were wrapped in the fluffy comforter I'd brought from my room and a few more layers of blankets, I sank into the soft mattress and soaked in the warmth of my boyfriends as the rain tumbled down the roof.

I drifted off to sleep content, but that ball of dread in my gut didn't ease.

One loud scream and a ferocious roar jolted us from our sleep.

My heartbeat thundered in my ears as we shot out of bed and rushed to get our clothes and weapons. Everything buzzed around me as worry gnawed through my brain. I hoped and prayed it wasn't my parents or Spencer who had screamed.

Micah threw the front door open, and shock slammed into me hard as a loud crack resounded from Ava's treehouse. Orange flames danced in the night, twisting and consuming the treehouse without mercy.

Thick black smoke rolled out of the windows and open door as more screams filled the air from inside. The fire engulfed an entire side of the treehouse before the thick sheet of rain went into a heavier downpour that made it dwindle, but not before a few flaming wood pieces fell onto the smaller supply shed below their home, eating through the roof in no time before it eventually stopped spreading, letting the rain put it out.

It took only seconds for us to snap out of the shock.

"Everyone stick together and watch out. That roar was the mountain lion. Weapons up." Micah was the first to descend, then Nathan, and then me. Calix helped me down until my hands gripped the wet wooden deck, but my fingers slipped from the side, and my foot missed the first peg leg.

"Tori!" Calix shouted, and I squeezed my eyes shut as I fell.

The rain pelted into my skin even as I fell with it, but two strong arms caught me before I smacked into the ground. "I caught you, darlin'. Can you stand?"

"Yes!" Gasping, I gripped Micah's arms as he and Nathan steadied me. "Thank you."

"Careful," Nathan called up to Calix, who successfully managed to get down the ladder.

Our shoes smacked against the wet muddy clearing as we ran toward the dwindling flames and thick smoke of Ava's treehouse where Benjamin and Sally stood in front of it, waving their hands and shouting their names.

Charles stumbled out, clutching his head before helping Ava get down the ladder, but she slipped on the last peg, and Benjamin moved forward to catch her.

Her eyes were frantic, and she trembled violently as she coughed. "We didn't close the bedroom window. I don't even know why it was open. It got in when we were sleeping and knocked over the candle by our bed. Jack's in there with it!"

Charles stumbled back in, and Micah cursed before gripping his axe tighter and kissing my temple. Then he stormed up the ladder to help.

My heart twisted in my chest as I watched him go, but I knew he had to help. They had to be okay.

There was a guttural growl before it went silent, and my entire body thrummed with unease as Nathan held me to his chest tightly.

It took too long for Micah to exit the treehouse with Charles and Jack behind him, and once they were all down safely, and Ava ran into her husband's arms, I ran into Micah's.

His arms caged around me safely, and he kissed my head. "I'm fine, darlin'. The mountain lion is dead. Jack killed it just as I got in there."

Relief plowed through me, but the dread only eased a little bit.

"Thank God for the rain," Benjamin muttered as he ran a hand down his face, staring at the supply shed.

Sally glanced at us before giving us a thankful smile. "Thank God you are going on a supply run tomorrow."

"It tried to run from the flames." Ava's voice cracked. "Since when do zombies run from danger if it meant infecting someone?"

"I don't know," Jack choked. "But I never want to encounter one like that again. It was too smart, and it was so fucking hard to kill."

Charles didn't say anything as he held onto his wife, but the look on his face showed the trauma they'd just gone through in there.

"You can stay with us," Sally offered.

The rain pounded down, making it to where everyone had to shout to be heard.

"Thank you!" Ava nodded at them.

Benjamin smacked Nathan's shoulder and squeezed. "Be safe, son. We're thankful it turned out this way and nothing worse."

"You too, Dad," Nathan murmured before we stood there for another minute, staring at the destruction of the treehouse.

It wasn't as bad as it could be, but it wasn't good either. The walls and roof were burnt down on the side of their bedroom and halfway into their living room.

"Let's get back in our home," Micah told us, and we all followed his lead to the treehouse.

I was thankful my parents and Spencer's treehouse was locked up tight, but I was also slightly happy they hadn't heard anything and had to witness that.

Nathan and Micah both helped me up the ladder and onto the deck safely before we went inside, and the warmth of the treehouse helped ease the bone-chilling cold from the rain and temperature. We discarded our soaked clothes and got into something warm and dry before we piled into Micah's bed and held each other tight.

I didn't want to think about how many more large predatory animals were zombified and intelligent roaming around us in the forest.

Solid sheets of rain poured through the night, battering the Oasis with fierce winds, but as we left the treehouse and headed to the clearing in the morning, the dark clouds parted for the morning sun that bathed our home in a gray light that showed the clear damage of Ava's treehouse and the supply shed.

"I hope the fire didn't give our location away to

any others in the area," Nathan muttered, but Micah shook his head.

"No. I don't think so. Not with the amount of rain last night. Anyone smart would be sheltered and unable to see it."

"But the roar and screams?" Calix asked with a shiver.

"The rain was so hard, maybe it drowned that out." Micah shrugged, but his eyes were tense as he surveyed the clearing and all the damage.

Benjamin and Dad came out of the supply shed with grim expressions.

"We were already low on medical supplies, but the fire got to most of what we had left," Benjamin informed us with a sigh. "Good thing you guys had planned to head out today. Temperatures are taking a nosedive, so take the tent. Shelter in any place you can on the trip."

Daisy and Jay strolled behind Mom and Spencer as they walked over with bags slung over their shoulders and baseball bats in their hands.

My brows raised as I tilted my head at them.

"We thought you could use the extra eyes. Safety in numbers, and quite frankly, they need to get their heads on straight. If they can't handle working with you as a team, they don't return back here." Benjamin crossed his arms as they came up, and Daisy bit down on her lip without saying a word.

"Okay," Nathan murmured, and everyone grew tense.

I knew that was the smart thing to do. I'd been able to live with them for so long because they mostly avoided me and never made the comments Daisy had since the horde. It was a toxic environment due to her constant issues with me, and the zombie apocalypse was bad enough.

"I wish I could go with you." Spencer threw her arms around me and hugged me tightly.

I let Nathan hold my golf club as I hugged her back. "I know. But Mom and Dad need your help with the animals. Besides, I think Ava could use your support right now."

She sniffled and pulled back with a nod. "I know, I know. Be safe out there, okay?"

"I promise."

"Here. This will be easier for now." Nathan fastened my golf club to my backpack.

"It takes two days to get to the town in the east," Micah explained, clasping his hands together. "We tried to go to the city in the west when we ran into the horde, but that trip is over a week long, maybe more. With the weather the way it is, we don't have that long so we need to go to the town."

"Are we taking the horses?" Jay asked, but Nathan shook his head.

"No horses. Better to go on foot in case we run into people. Raiders are notorious for only hitting towns and cities. Everything may be wiped out already honestly," Nathan answered with a frown. "Horses will make it more difficult to hide if we need to."

I swallowed a lump in my throat as Calix bumped his shoulder against mine.

"We should be back in four days then." Micah glanced around the group. "It's important to stay together and not wander off. I'll lead this trip, so what I say goes. Got it?"

Everyone nodded, including Jay and Daisy.

I just hoped this trip would go smoothly, but the ball of dread nestled in my lower gut told me something even worse would happen.

"Everyone double check their bags. Make sure everyone has enough water and food for a week," Nathan instructed as he slung his backpack off. "Have at least two extra sets of clothes and your weapons."

"I'll grab the tent." Micah went toward the larger shed. "Nathan, can you grab the rope?"

"I think Calix should grab that," he teased, and Calix's face went red before he stalked off toward the treehouse to get the rope currently tied to his bed frame.

Spencer grabbed my arm and pulled me away with a wide grin. "Bondage play?"

I groaned as I nodded, but I couldn't stop the smile from spreading over my lips. "Yes. Calix is surprisingly really into restraining me, and not just because of the lack of control."

"I'm jealous," she whined, and I frowned before pulling her into another hug.

"The world may have ended, but don't give up hope just yet. I'm sure someone is out there that you'll click with."

"If we ever find them," she muttered before pulling away and shaking her head. "I accept the loner life for a little longer."

"Can I talk to you?" Jay interjected, running a hand through his hair.

I glanced back and noticed Daisy was gone and raised a brow.

"Daisy went back to the treehouse to grab something," he explained.

"You can talk." I crossed my arms along with Spencer, who glared daggers at him.

"Look, I know since the horde came through things got worse with us and Daisy." His frown deepened, and he tapped his thumb on his palm. It was a nervous habit he'd had since I'd known him. "But it's because she's worried you still have feelings for me. I made the mistake of venting to her about the attention you were showing your boyfriends, and she took it as jealousy. My point is, she's not thinking rationally. I owe you so many apologies. I doubt you can forgive me, but I don't want us to be thrown out of this place because Daisy can't control herself."

I let out a long sigh. "Why do you care who I'm involved with now?"

"I don't. I mean, it's not about that. *I'm just sorry.*"

My head tilted as I processed what he had said, and once I did, a chuckle bubbled out of me. "Are you honestly apologizing to me just because you're worried about getting kicked out?"

His eyes widened as he shook his head. "No! That's not the only reason. I really do know how badly I fucked up. I shouldn't have ever gone there with Daisy without breaking up with you first, and I don't have an excuse for that. But I am sorry it hurt you."

I shook my head as my chest throbbed with a dull ache. "I've wanted an apology for years, but it feels flat. I don't think I'm ready to accept the apology, but I don't want any more bad blood between us either."

"That's fine," he said. "I am sorry, though."

I nodded and glanced at Spencer, who gave him a blank stare.

"What's going on here?" Daisy asked as she came over, but Jay wrapped an arm tightly around her.

I couldn't help but feel a little smug looking at the deep blues and purples surrounding Daisy's eye.

It looked painful, and I was starting to not feel sorry that I was responsible.

"I apologized for the past and everything else. We're dropping it, so you need to do the same," he hissed in her ear.

Her lips flattened into a line before she glanced at me and back at him. "I'm not apologizing."

"I wouldn't accept it anyway." I spun around with Spencer, and we went toward everyone else.

This trip was necessary, but I had a feeling Daisy wouldn't be able to keep her mouth shut. If she didn't, I knew the guys would have no problem leaving them in the town. I just hated how leaving them to face this world alone still bothered me after what they did.

22

TORI

The zombie's decomposing flesh flew from its face as my golf club cracked its skull, and it dropped like the bag of bones it was. "Two!"

"Three!" Calix shouted as his arrow split open another zombie's head, and I tried not to watch it splatter everywhere from the hit.

"Four and five," Nathan shouted as he shot two zombies, one behind the other, with one bullet.

"Six!" Micah's axe split open yet another undead skull.

Daisy swung her bat, cracking the head of a zombie without arms and knocking it on its back. She screamed as it groaned and tried to roll, but Jay smashed the head all the way in with his bat.

"Seven," he croaked, turning pale as he stumbled back from the seventh and last zombie in the spot we decided to set up camp.

We'd left behind the forest only about an hour ago, and the rolling hills were pretty, but the ground was hard and cold underneath our feet. The vast area was empty of everything and anyone except for the small group of undead we'd taken care of.

The sound of rushing water signaled the river just up ahead. I wouldn't have noticed the sound if not for Micah, and he was the one that suggested we run down and catch the attention of any zombie we could find around it.

In total, there were only seven that could be spotted.

We led them a good distance away from the river and the small level area next to it we planned to set up camp at.

"Let's head back and set up camp," Micah ordered gruffly, and nobody argued as we trekked toward the river.

The sun peeked through the gray clouds, casting a dull glow over the landscape. We went over the last hill that dropped straight down to the river, and I watched my step as I walked.

"Hold on to my arm, honey," Calix murmured as he held out his arm, and I grabbed onto him to help steady myself further.

"Thanks, Calix."

The water rushed through the earth, the surface

rippling and tumbling as it flowed. The leaves that lined the bank were brown and decaying over the mud. Chilly evening wind picked up my hair, stirring the strands in my field of vision as we stepped onto the flat, grassy spot near the water's edge.

I squeezed Calix's arm before letting go now that we weren't walking downhill.

"We'll start working on the tent." Micah tossed his bag and tent gear down as Nathan walked over to him. "Calix and Tori start a fire, and Daisy and Jay go looking for more sticks to keep the fire going."

"On it," Jay muttered, turning and walking down the bank with Daisy trailing behind.

They weren't completely terrible to deal with on the trip so far. I knew it was probably because of the guys. The first half of the day was tense, but the longer we were forced to deal with each other, the more bearable it became. That or it was just easier to ignore them.

The biggest downside of the two of them coming along was the fact that the tent would be shared by all of us. It was big enough for us not to be piled on top of each other. Walking a good distance through the day had tired us out, so I was hopeful there wouldn't be any arguing.

Calix and I kneeled close together as we found the driest spot near where Micah and Nathan were building the tent. The ground was still damp and cold, though, and the moisture seeped through my leggings as we got to work on the fire. Calix placed five or so smaller sticks on top of three larger pieces of wood and some dry nesting he'd found in a tree on the way here and placed it in a circle. He'd thought ahead and brought a few dry pieces of wood that he was able to find on the way. I handed him the flint and steel I carried in my bag, and he took it.

I loved the comfortable silence Calix and I fell into. It made me feel safe and accepted in a way I hadn't felt in silence with someone before, and I craved the feeling.

Tiny sparks flew from him working the flint and steel, and I leaned forward and blew gently, encouraging the wood to catch flame. After a few tries, the sticks crackled and burned, spreading over the kindling and heating the wood until it all started to catch fire.

"Fire's started," I called over to Micah, who gave me a grunt of acknowledgement. I turned back to Calix with a small smile. "Good job."

"You too." He got to his feet and held out his hand, and I took it as he helped me up.

"We have more sticks," Jay said as they walked back to us, both carrying armfuls of sticks.

"Place them next to the fire," Calix told him.

He did as he asked, and Calix and I went to help Micah and Nathan finish putting up the tent.

Once the tent was secured, we grabbed the canned food for tonight, and everyone's bags were placed inside.

We found a few dry logs and set them down next to the fire to sit on. The guys and I sat on one side while Daisy and Jay sat on the other.

"Do you think we could fish in the river?" Daisy spooned around in her can, the metal clanging as the utensil hit the side.

"We could in theory, but it's probably not a good idea," Nathan answered after he swallowed his bite. "With as many zombies that were walking in it, we'd be risking infection."

She frowned but nodded and glanced at me. "This reminds me of the time we camped out by the river on the farthest part of your ranch when we were teenagers."

The memories smacked into me hard, ones I'd tried to forget. I gave her a stiff nod. "Minus the fox den we stumbled upon."

She cracked a smile. "They trapped us in the tent all night, and your dad came looking for us the next morning."

"I'm sorry, but I have to ask," Nathan interrupted, setting his empty can down. "Why did *you* have an affair with Tori's boyfriend? Seems like you were close."

My heart thumped uncomfortably in my chest

as I frowned. I'd wanted to ask the same thing but never had the courage to.

Daisy's face twisted before she let out a groan. "Tori always got everything she wanted. I just wanted something too. She didn't even *appreciate* Jay. I honestly didn't think she'd care that much."

My lips parted as my eyebrows rose. Sure, I hadn't wanted to have sex with Jay after my surgery, but it was more to do with my lack of sex drive. I still showed him affection. The only time I complained to Daisy about him was when he would be distant with me, and looking back, she was the reason.

"Wow. Narcissistic answer," Calix muttered.

"So what's your reason?" Micah asked Jay with a scowl.

"She wasn't interested in sex anymore." Jay shrugged. "She went from doing it a lot to none, and it made me feel like she didn't like me anymore."

"I still showed you affection," I muttered bitterly, shaking my head. "I was still *trying* to make it work."

"But I also wanted kids, and you went ahead with the surgery even knowing that."

Anger swept through me, and I gripped the can so tight I shook. "I was in constant fucking pain, and I kept dealing with the pain until *you* told me if it would help maybe I should do it. And Daisy pushed me to do it too. I don't know why you use that as an excuse. You both just wanted each other. You should've broken up with me and dated her if that's what you wanted!"

"How long?" Nathan asked as the two of them slumped their shoulders and stared at the fire.

"A year," Jay admitted.

"A year?" I let out a whooshed breath. "How long after my surgery?"

"The day of." Daisy swallowed hard and glanced up, her eyes hardening. "I went over to be there for you when you were done with the surgery, and Jay was so upset over not having kids now. One thing led to another, and…"

"It never stopped because I fell in love with her," Jay finished.

It didn't hurt me to hear like I thought it would, but it did make my anger feel validated. They were two people who should've been honest and protected me. What they did reflected on them, not me.

"You two really are fucked up," Nathan muttered.

"We loved each other," Daisy told him, but he shook his head.

"We should get to bed before the fire goes out. I'll take first watch." Micah got up and unzipped the tent. "And for the record, if you hadn't fucked up, we wouldn't have Tori. You're idiots, but she's amazing."

"And for the record, lack of a sex drive is totally normal after a surgery like that," Calix told him. "Even if she didn't want sex, we would still be with her."

"It's just a really hot bonus that she has a healthy sex drive." Nathan winked before helping me up.

They kept their mouths shut as we all piled into the tent. I moved in between Nathan and Calix, and Daisy and Jay went as far as they could to the other side and cuddled up. Micah sat next to the three of us and looked out the small screen window.

Nathan's hand slipped up my shirt, and he rested his hand on my stomach, and Calix snuggled into my front, and I breathed in his clean scent.

Even with the conversation with Daisy and Jay, I fell asleep wrapped up in the comfort of the men who I knew cared for me while the river flowed outside the tent, a soothing presence in the darkness. I couldn't even stay angry knowing how long their affair lasted. Whoever they were in the past was irrelevant. I knew I didn't want anything else to do with them. I'd survive next to them, but that was it.

I just wanted to move forward with Calix, Micah, and Nathan, and that was exactly what I was going to do.

My Rotten Love Life

"Watch where you're going!" Calix snapped at Daisy, stumbling to the other side of me as he swatted at his shoulder where she'd bumped into him.

"Woah, chill." She held her hands up and raised her brow. "It's not like I have a disease or anything."

"But you could," I retorted. "He doesn't like being touched."

"I see him touch you all the time." She rolled her eyes.

"That's me. You're different. Respect his space."

"Whatever." She jogged up ahead of the group a bit.

The temperature dropped last night, and it hadn't come back up yet. The mottled sky ranged from dark gray to dirty white, and it looked like it was going to snow any minute. I hoped we could make it back before that happened, but that was unlikely. We still had to camp somewhere tonight before we could make it to town.

My heart dropped as we came up one of the lower hills. "Oh, shit."

Uncoordinated shuffling of the undead swayed back and forth, heading toward the direction of the town. It was a larger horde of at least thirty, and one look at Micah had my stomach twisting.

His lips were in a thin line, and his grip on his axe was so tight his knuckles were white. He scanned the area and paused toward the left. "Let's take that path. It's more southeast, but if we follow it, surely we'll find something. If that horde is going to the town, we may want to consider other options."

"But we need supplies," Nathan told him, running a hand through his hair. "What if the path leads to nothing?"

"Then we have to go northeast a bit until we can recognize the scenery toward town." Micah scratched his beard with a sigh. "We have no choice. We didn't bring enough ammo to take out a horde of that size when they aren't cornering us."

"Yeah." Nathan sucked in a deep breath before blowing it out and watching his breath swirl into the air. "You're right."

Changing course, we made our way toward the very small dirt path and kept our eyes on the horde that had been clueless of our presence.

It only took an hour before we came across a looming warehouse with broken boarded windows and crumbling walls sitting in the middle of nowhere.

"I've never seen this place on the map," Nathan

muttered before digging through his backpack and pulling the map out.

"There it is." Micah pointed toward the warehouse on the map. "It's weird that we've never noticed it before now."

"That's a tiny spec. I didn't think it was a damn warehouse. There could be a ton of supplies in there."

"But it could also have been scavenged already," Calix reminded him. "I mean, look at it."

"It could have been abandoned before the apocalypse." Jay shrugged.

"Maybe." Nathan stuffed the map back in his bag and put it back on his back. "Let's see if we can scope the place out. Just stick together and watch out for any people that could be hiding out in there."

"No kidding." Calix shivered. "It's probably a mess in there."

Micah led us carefully to the entrance, and with a deep breath, he went to push on the door, but it didn't budge. "It's locked."

"Let me." Nathan pointed his handgun at the lock, and we all stepped back before he shot it, and the loud metal clang made me jump. "You okay, killer?" He placed the gun back in his holster and glanced at me.

I nodded, my hand over my chest, and I felt my heart thundering beneath my rib cage. "Fine."

"Stay alert," Micah barked the order and kicked the door open with a loud creak.

We funneled inside, weapons ready. Our footsteps echoed within the large building, and the air was musty. The floor was littered with debris, but there were large shelves with a ton of different supplies stocked, kind of like a regular store but in bulk.

Thick layers of dust covered the packaged objects and totes, and the only sound was our footsteps and breathing.

After a few more minutes, we cleared the building. It was easy to do going aisle through aisle since there was no other room in the structure.

My muscles relaxed, and I let out a long breath after knowing we were alone and scanned the shelves. "There are so many supplies. How are we going to carry everything?"

"Just have to carry what we can, darlin'." Micah shot me a grin before his eyes widened.

He walked toward a section of axes and other tools that could be used for weapons. Rows of different size axes, arrows, baseball bats, and even a few machetes lined one side of the aisle.

We each started looking in the different aisles to see what we needed to bring, and I found an aisle with all kinds of fertilizers and seeds packed tight.

I reached out and grabbed a few spring seed packs, and excitement rushed through me. There were a ton of gardening supplies in the aisle too from tillers to water cans.

"Kind of an agricultural dream, huh?" Daisy walked down the aisle with her arms crossed over her chest and a pensive expression. "You really haven't changed much."

"I think I have." I shrugged, looking around to find a bag or something to put all the seed packs in to make it easy to carry back. "My love for gardening and self-sustainability makes more sense now that the apocalypse happened."

"Yeah." She smiled softly and glanced down. "I guess that's true."

I noticed a waterproof tote on the top shelf and stepped on the second shelf to give me a boost to grab it. The shelf creaked as I came back down, tote in my grasp, stumbling backwards and losing my footing.

"Shit, Tor!" Daisy reached out and grabbed my upper arm to stop me from falling into the shelf behind me. "Watch out."

I steadied myself while staring at her before she let my arm go and cleared her throat. "Thanks. That would've hurt."

"No problem."

"Guys, I found so many medical supplies! Hygiene, medicines, ointments, and literally anything else you can think of!" Calix's excited voice echoed through the warehouse. "Oh my

God!" He let out an excited squeal, making a giggle bubble out of me. "There's hand sanitizer! I haven't seen any since after the first year the apocalypse started! And it's *industrial size!* This is the best scavenging trip ever!"

Nathan's chuckle came after. "That's great, man! Gather as much as you can! There's some bags and even a wagon or two over here you can grab and fill up."

"Awesome!" Footsteps hit against the concrete floor as I assumed Calix rushed toward Nathan's voice to get a few bags.

I giggled and started putting the seed packs in the tote.

"You do look happier now," Daisy muttered, tucking a blonde lock behind her ear. "But I do love Jay. I really do."

My smile faded slightly, and I let out a sigh. "That's good. I'm not upset about you two finding happiness in each other. I'm upset about the way it happened. There was no excuse for it, especially with how long it lasted. It was more than disrespectful. It was just *wrong.* I will never understand how you don't get that."

"And I'll never understand why you chose him to date. I'll never understand why you continued to flaunt your relationship in my face even though I was uncomfortable."

"I never flaunted our relationship, Daisy." I

started grabbing more of the summer and fall seeds as well. I even threw in some sealed tight containers of other types of seasonal seeds that would be great to can next year after growth. "I was just in a relationship, and you were my best friend so you saw most of it. Plus, he asked me out. I even asked you if you cared, but you said go for it since you were dating his cousin."

"But you should've known I wasn't okay with it," she insisted. "We were *best friends, Tor!*"

"I'm not a mind reader." I set the bag down and turned to her with my hands on my hips. "If you had a problem with it, you should've told me when I asked. I wouldn't have said yes if you told me."

Her fists shook at her sides, and she turned her head away from me. "I probably should've. Maybe then we wouldn't be like this."

"Maybe." I frowned and turned back to the seeds, hearing her footsteps as she walked out of the aisle.

"There's so much ammo over here!" Nathan shouted from somewhere near the back. "This is fucking awesome!"

"I found some clothes and blankets!" Jay told us, and Daisy let out a squeal of glee.

"They have *dresses!*"

My lips curved into a smile as I continued filling the tote to the brim with seeds.

The Oasis did have a small garden a little ways

from Benjamin and Sally's treehouse, but it was nowhere near big enough to be able to start canning for the winter months.

I grabbed another tote and threw different types of fertilizers in it, listening to the excited chatter of the group. I couldn't believe all of these supplies had gone untouched for so long.

My parents would be so ecstatic to see all of this. I had to make sure to bring the seeds, fertilizer, and a few watering cans if I could find a big enough bag to store them in. Maybe I could find one of the wagons Nathan had mentioned.

Suddenly, there was a loud crash as the door was thrown open, and I knew it slammed off the wall just by the sound. Moans and groans reverberated through the warehouse, and my heart thundered in my chest.

Sucking in a deep breath, I placed the totes on the ground against the shelves and held my breath in as I moved toward the back of the warehouse, slipping behind the side of the aisle.

I jolted as my shoulder bumped Micah's, and he put his finger to his lips. I slapped my hand over my mouth when I looked forward. I took in the skeletal remains slumped against the back wall with a gun next to it. Its skull was shattered like a bullet went through it, but I didn't see the bullet.

Calix and Nathan stood behind another aisle a few rows down, and their eyes were calculated as they seemed to have a silent communication about *what to do*.

We had no idea how many zombies had come in, but it sounded like a good number of them.

My heart lodged in my throat as the moans got louder, and a small crash of something falling off a shelf caused them to groan and shuffle toward it.

"Jay! Move!" Daisy's shouts bounded through the structure, and my blood froze. "Jay!"

A louder series of groans sounded out.

My bottom lip quivered as I stared at Micah. His gaze hardened before he made eye contact with Calix and Nathan. They raised their weapons before quietly walking through the aisle I'd been in, and I crouched down to grab my golf club that I'd discarded when I noticed the seeds.

I peeked out of the aisle to see five zombies surrounding Jay and Daisy, but Jay was standing facing a zombie with its back to us, and his face was so pale.

Nathan raised his gun and started shooting them, but he let out a stream of curse words as a few changed direction toward us.

"It fucked up. Cover me." He smacked his palm against the gun.

Daisy yanked Jay's arm, but he wasn't budging. "Jay, it's not her anymore."

The zombie woman, dressed in a pencil skirt

and one high heel with a blouse on, limped closer before a growl tore from its throat.

I swung my golf club into the skull of the decayed zombie that had stepped in front of me, and its entire head flew off its shoulders before the body fell to the side.

My gaze swept back to Daisy and Jay just as the zombie lurched forward, and Daisy flung herself in front of Jay's stunned body.

An arrow whizzed through the back of its neck, but not before its teeth tore into Daisy's throat and landed on top of her.

My entire world froze as time seemed to slow. The zombie lifted from Daisy's gushing neck, her flesh between its teeth, and it glanced behind us.

It was a freshly turned zombie, and it was Jay's mother.

Turning back to Jay, it moved forward as Jay held his arm up, and her teeth sank into his forearm as a bullet hit her in the head.

"We need to amputate, *now*!" Micah barked an order, and Calix blinked at him.

"We don't know if that will stop the infection. That was only a rumor at the start."

"We have to try." My voice croaked, and I couldn't move my gaze from Daisy's body. Blood continued to pour from her neck all over the concrete. Her blue eyes were wide and starting to turn milky.

Calix shook his head before rushing to another aisle. "I'll grab a tourniquet and see if I can find a medical saw and a splint, but we need to watch him carefully the entire time. You need to have gloves and a mask on."

Jay's body was so pale he looked like a ghost, and he looked at his mother's corpse in horror. Blood trickled down his arm from the bite, but he didn't seem to notice. Janet was a prim and proper woman, so it didn't surprise me that she was dressed so fancy even in the apocalypse. She had always been cold to me, but even so, she didn't deserve to become undead.

Nathan got up and rushed over to the metal door he'd shot open and cursed. "It's a small horde."

"Fuck." Micah got up as Nathan held the door closed and barricaded it with a large metal cabinet that was sitting beside the door. "Let me find more to barricade it."

Daisy's fingers twitched before a gurgled moan left her.

My heart dropped as I leaned down and grabbed Micah's axe he'd left by Jay, switching my golf club for it. It would be easier to deliver the final blow since she was so newly turned. My stomach churned. "Jay…"

He barely blinked as his gaze was locked on his mother still.

Micah pushed another large piece of furniture toward the door Nathan held closed with the file cabinet, and Calix still hadn't returned from the aisle with the supplies.

I was on my own here.

Daisy pushed off the ground before stumbling back a few steps and locking her milky white gaze on me, her head tilted to the side as the gaping hole in her neck opened and closed with each step closer she took.

I gripped the axe tighter, and sweat dripped down my spine as my nerves seemed to heat my body. "I'm so sorry."

Her eyes widened, but she lunged forward, mouth open as her own blood still pooled inside it.

I swung the axe and embedded the sharp blade into the side of her skull, and a small groan escaped her mouth before her body convulsed. It felt like minutes watching the woman I used to call a best friend die for a second time in front of me. Then, she fell, and the axe slipped from my hands as it went down with her.

My throat burned as I held in a sob and stumbled backward. I'd just killed Daisy—zombie Daisy, but still. I'd killed plenty of undead corpses before, but I'd never put down anyone I knew when they were still alive. And Daisy was *just* talking to me in the aisle only minutes before.

"That should hold." Micah slapped the furniture holding the door shut. "At least until they move on."

"As long as they don't notice us in here," Nathan muttered.

"I have everything except a medical saw," Calix said as he came from the aisle but stopped short as he noticed Micah's axe in Daisy's skull and my probably horrified expression as I stared at her. "Oh, honey. I'm so sorry. I should've put her down before she could rise."

Calix set the supplies down next to Jay, who still hadn't budged, and then came over to me. His arms wrapped around me like a blanket of comfort, and I turned into his hold and buried my face in his chest.

"Damn it, darlin'. I'm so sorry," Micah murmured, going over to where Jay was with Nathan.

"You did good, Tori." Nathan quickly kissed the back of my head before moving over to Jay. "Alright, Jay, we need to amputate the bottom half of your arm before the infection sets in. Honestly, we may need to amputate the entire arm."

Jay didn't respond, and I was worried he was already dying.

"Entire arm," Micah rasped before getting up and grabbing a new axe after seeing his embedded in Daisy's brain.

Nathan used the tourniquet on Jay's shoulder before laying him down on the concrete, and as soon as his mother's corpse was out of his field of vision, his eyes fluttered shut.

"Gloves and masks," Calix reminded them, moving us a good ways away from them.

Nathan nodded and put gloves and a mask on, handing the extra to Micah as he came back with a saw and a new axe. Once they were covered, Nathan grabbed a bottle of whiskey Calix had brought with the medical supplies and shoved it in Jay's mouth, and Jay drank it like water without even opening his eyes. Nathan placed a piece of something in his mouth to bite on right after.

Everything else unfolded in front of me in a blur. I was watching it in the same room as it happened, but it didn't feel like I was. When Micah began to saw Jay's arm off, my hearing went static, and Jay's eyes flew open as he screamed. Even with his scream being muffled, it was still piercing.

Micah continued sawing his arm as Nathan jolted up to run and hold the furniture in front of the door as the horde outside began to bang on it.

The saw hit concrete, and Nathan rushed back over with the blow torch Calix had left in the pile. He put the flame against the head of the axe till it glowed a deep red, then passed it to Micah so he could cauterize the wound.

Jay's screams had stopped sometime between Nathan securing the door and heating up the axe since he'd passed out.

"There's antibiotics too," Calix murmured. "We have two bags full of pain relievers and antibiotics."

The horde finally stopped banging on the door a few minutes after Jay passed out.

"We need to finish gathering supplies. There are two decent-sized wagons in the back. Pile them up with as many bags of supplies as you can," Micah told us, and I nodded numbly before turning with Calix and going to retrieve all the supplies we could while I tried to block out the reality of what had just happened.

23

TORI

Sunlight streamed through the cracks of the wood holding the windows shut, and the groans and moans outside had seemed to have amplified since last night. I rolled over and realized all the guys had gotten up already from our spot in the back corner where we'd slept.

Jay was still asleep where we'd dragged him to, on the other side of the back of the warehouse, and I could see the sweat pouring off of him even from being a good ways away. Pushing up off the hard floor that was not softened by the sleeping bag, I made my way to the front of the warehouse, stretching out my sore muscles. I hadn't had time to process what happened yesterday, but I was thankful to be alive with my men.

Micah and Nathan had climbed up on the top of the shelves and were looking out the window, whispering to each other, and Calix rummaged through the wagons of supplies.

"I don't think Jay's going to make it," I murmured, barely recognizing my own voice.

The three of them whipped their heads toward me, but Calix was the one to come over and bring me into his warm embrace while the other two kept watch.

"I know, honey. He's running a fever, and he's been having seizures throughout the night. All signs of the zombie virus." He held me tighter. "We tried though."

"Isn't he supposed to have twenty-four hours? He's declined so rapidly. It hasn't even been twelve hours since the bite."

"Maybe the amputation sped it up, but I don't think it's due to infection from the amputation. I don't want to waste the medicine on him since he's going to die anyway," Calix explained, and I nodded.

"I understand that."

"So this is the zombie virus?" A rattled cough sounded from behind us, and we jumped to glance over at Jay, who stood in the aisle with a defeated expression. "I shouldn't have let my guard down. Because I did, Daisy…" He swayed on his feet as he clutched his chest.

"It was your mom," I murmured. "I can't imagine how hard that must've been."

He shrugged, letting out a weak chuckle before sliding to the floor. "You never liked her much anyway."

"I never wanted her dead, Jay," I snapped, and he nodded.

"So what now? Are you going to kill me before I turn?"

"Is that what you want?" Nathan asked, pointing his gun at Jay from his spot up by the window, and a jolt of surprise ran through me. But I did nothing to stop him.

Micah and Calix didn't look the least bit surprised.

Jay paused for a moment, but before he could answer, the door burst open, and a flood of zombies shoved the furniture out of the way, letting it clatter hard against the floor.

"Calix, Tori!" Micah shouted, and adrenaline slammed into me as Calix and I raced toward the aisle.

Both Calix and I were without our weapons, but we climbed the shelves just before the zombies started grabbing at the supplies on the shelves and throwing them to the ground as they tried and failed to climb after us.

I glanced over to Jay who was leaning against the shelf, and the zombies were just shambling past him.

My heart hammered in my chest, and static

filled my ears as I watched the zombies spill into the warehouse, moaning and groaning as they bee-lined toward us.

Nathan shot as many down as he could before he had to reload, and Micah shot arrows through the closest ones.

"Oh, my God. Is this it?" Fear clogged my throat at the wave of zombies as Calix wrapped me in his arms tightly, whispering words of reassurance in my ear.

There had to be at least forty of them in the warehouse.

"Calix, Micah, and Nathan... I don't know if there's going to be another time to say this, but—"

"Don't you dare, killer," Nathan gritted out, finger on the trigger. "You tell us when we get out of this mess."

"He's right, honey." Calix kissed my forehead.

Just as Micah and Nathan started making a dent in the numbers, gunfire sounded from outside.

Calix glanced out the window. "It's one woman, and she's headed this way. She's killing the zombies."

Micah and Nathan didn't stop taking them down, and there were only about fifteen left as a woman with two pistols barged into the warehouse and started shooting. She was dressed in all black as she gracefully dispatched the zombies with quick and deadly shots to the brain.

With the three of them, the horde dwindled to nothing in minutes, and my lungs finally filled with oxygen again.

The woman with shoulder-length straight black hair turned to us, and she wore a mask just like Calix's. "Glad I ran into you when I did."

"Not soon enough," Jay muttered bitterly.

She whirled around, gun pointed at his head before tilting her head and putting her guns back in the holsters. "You're not undead yet."

"Thanks for helping us," Micah said first, and we started climbing down carefully. The once clean warehouse was bloodied and filled with decayed bodies.

"No problem," she murmured, her gaze locked on one of the corpses. "My name's Akiko. I'm looking for my family. We got separated in town because of the horde, but I followed it in hopes of it taking me to my family. Janet was part of our group."

"Janet?" Jay coughed, pushing himself to his feet and holding on to the shelves for help.

"Janet was his mom," I added softly, and Akiko turned toward him with wide eyes.

"Jay? Your mom has been searching for you since the start. I met her two years ago when she and your dad ran into my group." Her shoulders slumped.

"Where's my dad?" Jay asked.

"He died only a couple of months after joining us. He got infected on a supply run." She shook her head sadly.

"Do you want to come back with us?" Micah offered. "You just helped save our lives. We would like to repay the favor."

She shook her head, but her eyes were grateful. "I may grab some supplies here, but I need to keep looking for my family. I appreciate the offer though."

"We wish you the best of luck," I told her softly, and she nodded.

I helped her get a few bags filled with different supplies, and she took her leave with a quick goodbye to us. I hoped she found her family.

Calix had checked over our wagons of supplies, and they were surprisingly fine after the mini-zombie-massacre. We gathered all of our equipment, and I had found a new golf club that was heavier than the old one. The older one was also starting to get worn out anyway. Even if there were better weapons to choose from, I felt the most comfortable with what I knew how to handle. Even if it wasn't the most practical weapon.

"We need to get going," Micah stated, his voice gruff and demanding.

Jay started coughing again, and he fell to the ground before blood sprayed from his mouth. "Fuck. I can't... It feels like my insides are melting."

"Jay…" I took a small step toward him, but he shook his head.

"Tor." He wheezed, coughing again, and it sounded like his lungs were filled with liquid as he spoke. "You were never as affectionate with me like you are with them. Maybe it did make me jealous. Daisy thought so… I'm sorry, but I loved Daisy… Glad you found something too." He fell face first into his blood and convulsed violently before his eyes shot back open.

Unlike Daisy's milky look in her eyes, Jay's were filled with blood. It struck fear into my chest, and I readied my golf club as he pushed off the floor and came at me. I swung the golf club, and his head snapped to the side with a crack before he fell to the ground, but his hands twitched.

I stumbled back into strong arms, and a bullet shot through Jay's head the next second.

"I got you, darlin'."

"You did great," Nathan assured me, tucking his gun away.

"Let's go home." Calix grabbed one of the wagons as Nathan grabbed the other, and my mind was jumbled as we left the warehouse and my two ex-somethings behind.

The rest of the day was a blur, and we made it to the river before the sun set. The sky was a dark, menacing gray, and the air was still. The river flowed with small ripples, unlike the rushing it had done just a couple of days ago after the rain.

As Micah and Nathan set up the tent and Calix helped the fire roar to life, a gust of cold, bitter wind blew through, and the first snowflakes of winter danced and twirled down from the dark sky. The snowfall was light as we sat down around the fire and filled our stomachs with canned soups, but as we entered the tent for the night, the flakes got heavier and heavier.

I curled up between my men, soaking up their body heat. "Thanks for being here," I murmured.

Calix's lips pressed against my temple. "Wouldn't want to be anywhere else, honey."

Micah's beard scratched my cheek as he leaned over Nathan and kissed my lips. "Always here for you, darlin'."

Nathan buried his face in my neck and kissed it gently. "Always."

"Get some sleep. I'm taking first watch, but we may have to travel in the dark if the snow starts to pile up more," Micah rasped, but I had already started to drift asleep.

Nathan woke me up early in the morning before the sun rose. The snow had created a thin blanket over the landscape, and the temperature was well below freezing.

We bundled up with the new coats that Jay had found at the warehouse and Calix had remembered to pack and headed back to the Oasis with the two wagons filled in tow.

Snow crunched underfoot, and the sun had finally started to peek over the horizon.

"Are you okay, honey?" Calix's voice was soft and concerned, and I lifted my shoulders in a shrug.

"Daisy and Jay used to be the most important people in my life, but then they betrayed my trust and ruined my perception of them." I blew out audible breaths. "I'd mourned who they were to me after that. Their deaths were nothing I had wanted to happen, but it doesn't hurt anymore than it did when I lost them in the past."

"You still put down people you knew in life," Micah rasped. "Even if you held contempt for them, it's hard. It's okay to let yourself process and feel it."

"But if you have nothing to process about it, that's okay too. Just because they're dead doesn't mean they didn't suck," Nathan added helpfully, but Micah elbowed him in the arm.

"I've fallen so hard for you guys." My stomach fluttered with a sense of belonging. They all stopped walking and stared at me, and I paused before tugging the cotton hat over my ears. "What?"

"Is that your love confession?" Nathan dropped the wagon handle and moved forward. "Because now it's not life or death. You can't take it back if you say it."

Heat flushed my cheeks as I nodded. "Yeah. I guess it is. I mean, I *do* love you. All of you. I can't imagine life without you."

Nathan swooped forward, smashing his lips to mine before pulling back. "I love you too."

Micah caught my wrist and tugged me into his chest. "I love you, darlin'. Figured it was obvious by now."

"I love you too, honey," Calix murmured sweetly, and his eyes were glossy as he cleared his throat as we started our journey home.

We reached the Oasis when oranges and pinks blazed through the horizon, casting a warm glow over the heavily blanketed snow on the ground. The air was bitingly colder than it was when we started, and large flakes continued to fall from the sky, whipping back and forth from the gusts of wind.

Nathan and Micah pulled the wagons through

the couple of inches of snow with little problem, but when the treehouses came into sight and Bane started growling, my heart filled with relief.

Bane snarled and dug his bony paws into the snow, trying his damnedest to infect us, and Micah let out a rough sigh.

"Sometimes I wish I could pet him, but that's not Bane anymore. It's just another rotten corpse."

I reached over and squeezed his hand. "But Bane had you in his life to comfort and love him. That's not Bane."

"I know."

"Tori!" Spencer's voice was the first to greet us as she rushed through the snow and threw her arms around me, stumbling us back a few steps as she hugged me. "We were *so* worried about you guys with the snowfall." She pulled back, and her gaze widened. "Woah! That's a lot of supplies. That's good. We definitely need some good news here."

"Rebuilding seems to have started," Micah commented, glancing at the now rebuilt shed and still-being-rebuilt treehouse of Ava's.

"Yeah, but there's a lot more happening," Spencer murmured sadly as Benjamin came over.

"You're back early with supplies." He clasped his son on his shoulder and regarded us with kind eyes. "I'm glad. Did the other two cause issues?"

"Not quite," Nathan said with a rattled sigh. "Daisy was killed by a zombie, and Jay was bit but even after an amputation, he succumbed to the virus."

Benjamin's eyebrows rose in surprise, but he nodded. "I'm sorry. We had the same luck here. Charles hid a bite from that infected mountain lion until it was too late. We realized what had happened just before he passed, and Jack had to put him down. Ava's a wreck."

"Damn it." Micah ran a hand through his hair.

"Ava's up in the treehouse with Sally," Benjamin explained with a sweep of his arm. "Jack's been doing any and everything to keep his mind off it. He's almost finished with the treehouse."

"Wow." My voice cracked.

Life was never guaranteed, but so much death around us made me realize just how true it was.

"We need to shower," Calix said, and the group agreed.

Spencer knocked her shoulder with mine. "Come up to our treehouse for a bit after? I'd like to catch up."

"Sure, Spence." I gave her a soft smile as she bounded up to the treehouse.

"She's a good sister," Micah told me, and I nodded.

"She really is."

"I'll help Dad get these wagons into the shed then come back with clothes. Go ahead and shower.

We've had a tough trip." Nathan cupped my face in his hands and kissed my lips softly.

Calix, Micah, and I made our way to the shower shed and discarded our clothes as we let the water warm up.

Goosebumps pebbled my skin even as we stepped under the stream of warm water, and they grabbed the soap before lathering me up.

Their touches were gentle and caring, and while Micah washed my body, Calix washed my hair. When I was rinsed, I did the same for Micah.

As I washed Calix, Nathan stepped in with a pile of clothes in his arms. "Hey, can you wash me too?"

"Get in here." I leaned Calix's head back slightly and rinsed the suds out of it, threading my fingers through his hair until it was soap free.

Nathan stripped out of his clothes and came into the shower as Calix and Micah left it, and I soaped my hands up before washing and rinsing him clean. He backed me up against the shed wall before leaning down and kissing my lips as he turned the water off and pulled away. "Thanks, killer."

Calix handed me a fluffy towel, and we all dried off before getting dressed again.

They walked me to the bottom of my parents' treehouse, each kissing me on the head before heading back to ours.

My Rotten Love Life

"We'll be waiting for you!" Nathan called after me as I climbed up the tree onto the deck.

I waved back at them before taking a deep breath and opening the door to the treehouse I realized I hadn't even been in.

It hadn't been that long since we came to the Oasis, but even so, I'd been so wrapped up in Calix, Micah, and Nathan that I hadn't had much time with my family. I knew it was normal, especially with everything we had to do, and at that time, I had been avoiding Daisy and Jay, but I still missed my family.

Spencer's eyes lit up as she jumped off a beige sofa and came to drag me to sit down. "You need some sister time, Tori. Fess up. I know everything's been getting to you."

Sucking in a deep breath, I unloaded everything that had happened since coming to the Oasis up until now. My parents came in mid-way through my explanations, and my family did nothing but offer me reassurance.

I didn't realize how much I needed their acceptance and love until that moment.

Everything might have been hard now, but I still had my family and my boyfriends. That was a lot more than most people had, and I was eternally grateful.

24

TORI

I pulled the door shut as I stepped into our treehouse, and warmth from the wood stove fell over me like a blanket.

Shrugging out of my coat and scarf, I kicked off my shoes and gave a small wave to the guys who were sprawled over the sofa and recliner before making a bee-line to Micah's bedroom where I stripped off the rest of my clothes and snuggled under the blankets.

Their footsteps were right behind me before they each sat on the bed, making it move with the movements.

"How was the talk with your family, darlin'?" Micah's raspy voice sent tingles down my spine.

"It was good," I murmured against the soft pillow. "We rehashed everything since we left the ranch, and I think we all needed it."

"Good. I'm glad you were able to be there for each other," Calix said softly. "Are you hungry?"

I shook my head. "I ate at my parents'."

"We could always have some fun." Nathan scooted toward me and slipped his hand down my spine, slowly pulling the blanket back. "Take our minds off the past couple of days…"

"You think so?" I flipped over to my back, and the air of the room skimmed over my bare breasts, making me tremble.

"You're stunning," Micah rasped as I glanced up at him with hooded eyes.

"Hold on!" Calix stuttered. "I'll do my best, but we need to mouth wash and wash our hands right now before this starts."

"You'll join?" My gaze snapped to Calix, and his face was red as he nodded.

I thought getting up and having us all wash our hands and teeth plus mouthwash would've killed the mood, but it didn't. If anything, it added to the anticipation of having my men and touching them freely.

Nathan was the last of us to come back into the bedroom, and he had a small tube of something in his hand with a devious smile playing on his lips. "Hear me out…"

"Is that lube?" Micah chuckled.

"Of course it is." Nathan winked. "If Tori was

up for it, I figured we could take her at the same time."

My mouth fell open as heat pooled in my core. "What do you mean by that?"

"I was thinking I could try to take you from the back while Micah took you in your pretty pussy."

"And Calix?" My voice was husky.

"He could fuck your mouth."

"From the back?" Calix paled. "Like in her butt? There are *so* many germs there!"

"Well, where else would you like us to try it? Both in her pussy?" Nathan rolled his eyes with a pause. "Actually…"

"Yes! That would be way better than her ass, Nathan," Calix hissed.

Nathan's brow rose slightly before he regarded me with mischievous eyes. "What do you say, killer? Want to try to take us both in your pussy?"

"Would that work?" My heart raced in my chest as my desire filled every bit of me, pushing me to say yes to anything the three men in front of me wanted to do.

"We can make it work," Micah confirmed, and I nodded my head in awe as I watched him strip and release his hardened cock.

He pinned me to the bed and ran the engorged tip of his dick through my slick folds and moaned. "Already wet for this, darlin'?"

"Yes," I gasped before his lips took mine. His

kiss was possessive and consuming, and he gripped me tightly before flipping us over and impaling me on his steel cock.

"Micah!" I cried out as he filled me completely, stretching my walls in a way that sent pleasure crashing over me.

"Good girl. I love seeing you on top of me like this," he rasped, fingers biting into my hips as I started to rock back and forth.

Pleasure burst in my nerves with every motion, and my head fell back as a low moan left my lips.

The bed dipped as two hands circled from my back and cupped my breasts. "How wet is she?" Nathan tweaked my nipples, making my pussy clamp down harder on Micah as I rode him.

"Fuck." Micah let out a breathy moan. "Soaking me."

"Good," Nathan purred before licking the side of my neck, and his hands moved from my breasts, making me whine. "Don't worry, killer. I haven't even started." One hand splayed over the back of my head, forcing me down against Micah, and his other hand felt around my already stuffed hole.

Another whimper tore from my throat, but Micah's hand moved from my hip to my breasts, playing with my nipple and sending another wave of ecstasy through me.

It felt so good, but I needed *more*.

Micah tensed before he pulled out, and I

opened my mouth, but his mouth covered mine and swallowed my protest.

"God, this feels weird," Nathan murmured before both his and Micah's cocks slipped inside me, coated in even more lubricant to make getting inside easier than I'd imagined.

"Oh, fuck," I moaned like a mad woman, breaking my kiss with Micah and arching my back as they bottomed out inside of me.

My pussy was *so* full. Fuller than I'd ever thought possible, and the stretching of it wasn't painful at all. It was blissful, and it made every part of my body cry out for a release.

"You okay, honey?" Calix's concerned voice did little to bring me out of the lustful haze I was drowning in.

I nodded lazily and reached out for him, and he hesitated.

"Calix, sweetheart, please," I whimpered, still basking at the fullness I felt.

His composure broke as he shuffled onto the bed and cupped my face with his hands before pressing a soft kiss to my lips. "I don't know what I can do."

He was kneeling on the bed, and his cock was fully erect and weeping from the tip.

"I do." I curled my fingers around his shaft before leaning slightly over, pulling his dick toward me until he filled my mouth.

My pussy tightened around Micah and Nathan as I sucked gently on Calix's cock, and he moaned.

"Taking all three of us so good, darlin'."

"So fucking pretty," Nathan murmured.

They started to move inside of me, and pure ecstasy shot sparks through my body with each synced thrust.

I moaned, my lips wrapped around Calix's shaft, and I shook with pleasure as my climax built up.

Calix's hips tensed before he let out an uncontainable moan and spilled cum down my throat. "Sorry, Tori."

I swallowed it, and he slipped out of my mouth before sitting back on his ass and staring at me in awe.

"Don't be. I liked it," I moaned, my head falling between Micah's head and shoulder as they picked up their speed, thrusting into me until Nathan stilled and came as he moaned my name.

Stars combusted behind my eyelids as I trembled at the continuous waves of pleasure washing over me, and I squeezed down on their cocks even harder.

"Holy fuck, I love you guys," I mumbled in a haze.

"I love you too, honey." Calix said as his gaze bore into me.

"I love you too, darlin'." Micah pumped into

me a few more times before he came with a grunt, wrapping his hand in my hair and pulling me in for a kiss.

Nathan pulled out first, dropping a kiss to my shoulder. "I love you, killer."

Calix threw himself into overdrive with cleaning the bed and ourselves. Almost an hour later, we each fell into the clean sheets he'd had on standby with a new blanket, wrapped up in each other's arms.

I knew the zombie apocalypse wasn't going to be easy, but having these three men by my side made everything else bearable.

A THICK BLANKET OF SNOW COVERED THE CLEARING except for the bonfire that crackled and snapped as fire roared within it. We all stood around the fire, eating the first fresh meat we'd had in months. Thanks to Micah, who had stumbled upon an uninfected deer.

It'd been two weeks since our trip to get the supplies, and winter had hit in full force.

Ava and Jack were still healing from the loss of Charles, and so was the Oasis. I was still healing from the loss of Kovu, and I had come to terms with what had happened with Daisy and Jay.

The Oasis had changed my life, not without losses, but the outcome was brighter than I ever could've imagined.

Our livestock were happy and thriving here with their new homes, and my parents had remembered the heaters for winter so they wouldn't be cold. We had enough food and seeds to last, and we were planning for a fruitful future.

We would have to scavenge a few more times to the warehouse come spring, but we were so grateful for what we had.

Spencer bumped my shoulder with a smile. "I'm so happy we left the ranch."

I glanced around the fire at everyone mingling, and my heart swelled as I watched my boyfriends talking with my parents. "I am too, Spence."

The Oasis and those in it had become our family, and I was so thankful for the way everything turned out.

25

TORI

EPILOGUE

One year later…

I SAT CROSSED-LEGGED ON OUR LIVING ROOM FLOOR and tilted my head. "Yeah, I'll buy it."

Nathan groaned and pouted at me. "Come on, killer. You can sell it to me."

I pretended to think about it for a second, tapping my finger on my chin before grinning. "Nope."

He groaned dramatically, and Calix and Micah chuckled at him.

"Don't laugh. She's bought one of all your properties too," Nathan grumbled as he rolled his dice.

The groans and moans from the horde outside turned to white noise. It was day two of the horde, and it was much bigger than it had been last year.

Within just a year, we'd turned the Oasis into a completely self-sufficient sanctuary. We didn't even *have* to go scavenging anymore unless we wanted to.

The only downside was that the zombies had seemed to get smarter, but so had we. And so had the remaining animals in the forest.

We had even run into Akiko earlier this year at the warehouse again, and she'd had a man Spencer's age with her. She hadn't found her family, so she opted for retiring to the Oasis with us.

Spencer and the man, Keith, had developed a romantic relationship, and I couldn't be happier for her. Keith was a good guy from what we'd seen so far, and he'd moved into my parents' treehouse with Spencer already. Akiko stayed in the treehouse with Ava and Jack, who were only now starting to find their footing without Charles.

Calix leaned over and kissed my cheek. "Can you believe this is how we met?"

"I was just thinking about it." My body buzzed with belonging. "I'm so happy I found you guys."

"We are too, darlin'." Micah took his turn with a soft smile my way.

"Even though we were the ones that found you." Nathan winked. "I couldn't be more grateful we noticed your ranch that day."

Life in the apocalypse was brutal, but with my men and family at my side, I could survive anything, and really, that was all I could ask for.

ACKNOWLEDGEMENTS

My Rotten Love Life was such a fun book to write! I went down the rabbit hole of reading whychoose zombie apocalypse books last year, and this story popped in my mind to write. I was so happy to finally make the time to write it.

Tori and her men were so comforting even in an apocalyptic world!

Jacob, my husband. Your support and listening to my all crazy ramblings are so very appreciated. I love you!

Sam, my PA and Alpha reader. I appreciate everything you do for me and for you messaging me to make sure I'm okay. You are amazing!

My Alpha Readers. You are essential to all of my stories! I love you so much and love how much you love the characters I create! I also love how you fight over the guys! ;)

My Beta Readers. You catch all the mistakes I didn't, and you are so motivating. I love how involved you get in the story and all your suggestions!

My readers. Without you, all this wouldn't be possible. You're so appreciated and loved!

LYRA WINTERS

Welcome to the realm of complex plots, relatable characters, magical worlds, and 3+ swoon-worthy men that you don't have to choose between!

I'm thrilled you stumbled upon my books and the worlds I've created! There's just something about the paranormal side of things when romance and spice are added that makes me feel warm and fuzzy inside!

I'm a twenty-something Kentucky woman who has escaped fully into the book world. When I'm not typing away on my laptop, daydreaming book ideas, or devouring stories, I'm taking care of my two spunky daughters and loving on my dreamy husband.

Fun facts: At least one man in the relationships I write is inspired by my husband. I'm also addicted to Coca-Cola, 2000s rap music, and bubble baths.

Don't be afraid to lose yourself in the escapism of this genre.
XOXO,
your friendly neighborhood paranormal why choose author

FOLLOW ME FOR UPDATES!

Join Lyra's Labyrinth on Facebook
Visit my website to join my Newsletter
Follow me on Amazon for new release alerts
Follow my page on Facebook
Follow me on Instagram
Follow me on Pinterest
Want signed copies and/or fun SWAG from my books? Check out my Etsy shop!

ALSO BY LYRA WINTERS

Fate Hollow Academy

Term 1

Term 2

Term 3

Term 4

My Rotten Love Life

My Rotten Love Life

Sons of Satan

Corrupting Lust

The Crimson Demon

Crimson Death (Prequel)

Crimson Tears (Book 1)

Crimson Kiss (Book 2)

Crimson Soul (Book 3)